THE SWORD, THE WORD, AND THE WRITINGS

THE SWORD, THE WORD, AND THE WRITINGS

E Lloyd Kelly

CONTENTS

THE SWORD, THE WORD, AND THE WRITINGS

Book #3 from the REAL INKY TRAIL SERIES.
Description
The Sword, the Word, and the Writings is book number three in the "Real Inky Trail" book series. This is a fictional story, based partly on some facts and current affairs, and set in Cekkoland of the KDs. The names and characters depicted in this book are fictitious and not to be construed as being real or associated with any actual person, living or dead.

This story is told from a Carib-Jamericanadian perspective. In a richly blended language mix of nonsense talk, sensational spelling, double entendre, poetry, and seasoned with snippets of Jamaican Patois inserted here and there throughout, as may be found fitting. Yeah, man, a Jamaica yaad mi come fram, sorry, I meant to say; I'm Jamaican born and bred, okay? Yes, wordplay is the order of the day around here.

The Meeting in the Sphere

They were all there, worshipping the memory, and merry-making, honoring the lifestyle and spirit of their elders, the ancient. Caring about nothing other than their children, the innocent. Basking in the glories of those who had long walked the way, even way before their time, and would have served their time and gone. Those who had lived and taught those golden ways, and the ancient custom of the ancestors to the offspring... naves. Those have now been passed on by way of the graves. Then came the un-graving, just to get things even. Then came the other men, with the sword and the word in hand. The sword was in the right hand, and the word in the left hand did leave a lasting impact on the left wing; thereupon, the writing on the walls of that circular lot. Deep wounds that those of the square way could not retrace. Not that they would even contemplate such an act. Nor were they ever going to make a move on anything the likes of that, but... They were out searching for one when they found this promised land. That which he, yes, that man, found it there heavy under the palming hand of a circular man. In that very place where the legs of his Larrie ancestors once stood upon the stands and walked the walk thereupon. But he came in; that squared-faced man, along with all his thieving companions. He then took off his caped boots and sat down, cute after he was done tasting the loot, all coming to him at the hands of Lars's own easy and giving suits. Got the sword in his right hand, and a word in the left, you bet. Wanted to feel his soul atop their sand before getting around to giving the command to the rest of his clan, to fix them up nice and easy. Yes, Aunt

Enid. Readying them up for the meeting of the man's mind, yeah! He would have done it every time, that same one whom they were so inclined to dine. Yeah, the same offspring kind from the Larried Vine did. They wined and dined with him. He whom they did not know aforetimes, even. Before he's done, though, with kneading away at all of that dough. They are sure to know whatever "knowing to do" will be left in them, you, and all of your kind, too. For a short spell, they did scare the sheets out of the Square Kings' sleep. Wiped the smile off his grinning half-white teeth, then tossed it into the pit of the wastebasket. Happened when he first sat down to eat and was forced to watch over it. Yes, upon the story. He'd wanted to see the glory of the ancestors' story, to partake of the service and sacramentary. The offerings as offered up to their gods in worship momentarily, but — "Oh, look at the Hut." He was heard grumbling this in his gut. In trembling, though, did he not tremble, and put on the squared deceitful face of the humble?

"No-o!"

"Yes, he did," tumbling down upon him and the rest of them there, with a pile of snake oil-like nutty buddies, my dear, tooting and arguing out all the arguments. Got them believing for a while that he was genuinely docile, by covering up the brute square there under a plastic smile, Aunt Sue. Then quickly turned around to go and shake up a brew. He took to shaking his hand at a shaky plate. Shaking his lying pancake baking palm oil in front of their circular style. Those who were there, misreading the profile, would have done so to their exile. Cast out in an unceremonious style to go off exhuming kingdom bones below the river Denial. By the time he was good and done, and gone back to his first place, in the "frigid zone." Way up there, where he still stands up tall and calls it all his home. On top of what he'd dragged a backpack and then stacked and piled it from under some circular tailbone. The entire earth is his home, even now, and barring none. As for their gods who had served them then, like, from when they were glad, and mirth remained. Well, up until those squares were to hop on in, to rock and roll all over their soul, again. Whatever happened to them, yes, those good, godly friends? He took those gods and tossed them away, then gave them a bag of hay upon which to go kneel and pray, worshiping like sheep. Among other bits of soft-spoken, easy-flowing downhill sleet. Ever since then, they have been doing it, my friend. Why, oh why, my little bunny rabbit? Why can't you do it? I mean, like, quit?

The old man saw them coming when they first came in, sliding squarely upon regular slimy skating gear, as they are known. The juice, my youth, as picked up and brought in from way up there under his walking boots, that is the truth. Too much of such over on that side shout, he could not avoid it on the way out. So, he slid right in on them. As for them, those Larrie gentlemen? They were never the same again. They roped him in with their warm, smoking chimney, shining beauty, and splendor. Came he not knocking at their window, and hopping in through their wide-open door? Yes, that was it. They would have seen their mighty men and their godly friends, yes, them. They would have seen them again, like, no more.

...

"War, war, and yet more wars," was what they heard coming into the car across the notes of the bar player's guitar. "This is war, between the squares and the circulars." The cubes, however, were somewhere in there among those squares on the river. To be fair to them, they were top-tier children, but they were sitting there just like always, yes. They had always been sitting there, cozying up and over in an old rocking chair and savoring the fouled-up musky air. Not much to do over there other than to screw and unscrew the bottled beer. Just like they already knew that they should never do, yes, my dear. But screwing hard at the screw, they did. And "pop," it came to the top of the liquor jar, as they swallowed hard at the bar brawl. Pausing for just a while from singing along to the songs of the Pee on no man who was there playing a gig at the barstool stand. But for a while, he didn't smile. Neither did any of his raving admirers because they thought he was pausing, giving them laughs in fine style and wasting time gazing up at the singing, shining star. Those fastened fast to the blanket there, yonder far. But, in reality, it was something quite amazing to him and me. To the rest of them, too, in the end. Because, in looking around, in those places that they did not know before the times of their homely faces, bright or brown. They were to see some possibilities out there. Yes, they did. Out there in those very places near where they lived. There were some trees, the evergreen kind. Outer yet further, too, as far as the eyes could see me through the scenes. Like, somewhere out there over the shoulder, when one turns the head to look at you, son of the Deans. "No, not at me, but…"

Anyways, there were mighty wooded forests out there, and yet other green trees. A called possibility his lying eyes would have come to see, seen?

"Seen."

"Yeah, man, Yardie sin ting, or something." He was sucked in right away. Like, sucked in to become a wandering form, from that very day on, and hence…

Then, look, over there is Lars. Shortened and Circular. Just the way they always are, in particular. They, too, were there, gazing, spending many odd days in and out. Out in the open, looking about, and upward bent. You know, like, they were there, bending their necks backward, while watching the stars and tracking the herd. They sure liked to have things staying just the way they already are, like his way. "My way," he says, "or no way at all." Yeah! That will take him far, you know, because he's a Lar, and everybody already knows the score: that every Lar is a star. "Ruff and buff," and that's surely going to be more than enough for those Larried Lars and company. But the first casualty of any war, as was to be discovered by those from afar, is the truth. The squared one, that brute, quickly majored in this sphere, true? "True." Not the youths, though. Youths, just the same as you. Like, him too, yeah! I'm pointing him out to you. Can you not see him walking by the old man sitting there in his lone shoe? "Yeah, man!" That would be him. He, just like all the rest of the Larried family, majored in very little, if anything at all. So, it was the city of squares over there that would have managed to major in there. Majoring in the major things fast and fair, like quickly learning and getting to know how to manipulate and twist other people's truths. All of his other fine things are cute, too. But he continued doing his studies over you to come up with several versions of the other man's boot for him and his buddies, Boo-boo. They also learned how to create their truth by doing so. Like, how to pass those things off as something soothing. Or something else could have been brewing. That, too, would have been to their suits, Sue Hingh. Things such as someone else's truths. Even worse than that, he could pass them off as the ultimate truth, no? "Yes." They quickly noticed a tooth, and while the Notice families were there giving ears to the mute, they'd picked up a note that said: People spoke just like Pickney, yes, my child, as in childhood, children wrote and read, for the most part. They liked to worship stars and throw spikey, pointed piercing darts. They were rather spiritual, too, in the natural arts. The Lars are mostly so, so smart. Wink-wink. I'm here thinking of linking up the car to the shining star and going right by him to take a spin over the rim, no? Look at him, a real whim, no? Yes, let's go. So, the squares drew themselves nearer. Then go on out to out-steer them, and her. To make something up for them, somewhere up there, where it occurred...

"Where, when? You mean, like, like, out there?"

"Yes, Sir, Mister Pointy Finger." He makes gods for them up there, somewhere up in the air, and sticks them there to linger, somewhere between the right and the left ear symbols. Other gods, too, he made them all new. Other gods than those of theirs whom the Lars would have known and worshiped aforetimes, from afar. Out of their godly fear and favor to her. The Squares gave them something to wake them up. Then send them off to the workshop, and to "wonder-working worship," and they did. Didn't they give good, godly gifts? Yes, Siree, yes, they did.

Meanwhile, the circulars were there, busily majoring around in a round of beer at the bar of golf. Gulping down the gullible in believing in such. Like, believing lies, even. Lies chiefly, Ben.

"Why, but why?"

"Why!" Did you ask my guy friend? Well, listen up while I sell you a pen. The bigger a lie bends, the more likely those circulars are going to believe in it. Suits the squares very fine, fren-a-mine. You're certainly a good friend to me and mine, but then. Along with the rest of them, like, with their other kind squared friends. He went out and about, scouting. That was when he'd scouted them out and spent on the wee win; yes, he did. He would have spent the time and the necessary overtime. Creating signs and lie-lines, among other tried things, and his alibis. Things like strong and beautiful thighs to show off before their eyes. Tied up in military things and hung them on a long string. Then neck-laced them somewhere below the teeth of the heathens. Then went out further and started building big and scary buildings that were designed to get the other wide-eyed void, you know them! Yes, I wouldn't have lied while sitting below them on the wrong side. "You mean, those same rounded circulars from the other side?"

"Yes." Got them trembling at the knee dem them de de-dumbed dumb. Dimensions tumbling down, to keep them running and rolling around. With momentum, too, like toot, toot, toot tooting towards nothing new. Nothing else needed to be done, no need to. They're circular after all, round around there they are, remember? So, the Squares just keep on keeping them in subjection and submission, believing in lies unlimited, and believing yet the more, "yuh simi, kid?"

"Yes, I can see you."

Well, nice. Because "I've got to be sure," he snores, "to be delivered from the iron ore, this gripping grip of this other odor; the lip-sticking grips of this squared person in proper. Since I can't do it for myself, then there has got to be someone else, somewhere else, living or dead. Someone from somewhere other than here on these old dusty belts, beneath my bed. Yes, that might be the 'someone' personality who will do it for me. Someone more or less like a good, Godly, god-fatherly person, probably. Even his sweet, untouched yet touchable mother, yes, maybe. Since I've already given up on the godly goodness of my forefathers' family witness, or was forced further to give up and forget the order. Of all of them, even." So ordered by the other orders that were sent down from the other men in Eden to us, and them. The harder they came, the harder we went. Since I've already done all that. Then, I had better be sure to hold fast to the gods I've already bought. Like the ones that he has given to me and taught. I must go on and believe in them, with all of me, Ben. With my whole heart, too, who knew? Yes, "I must believe that he will deliver, rescue, and save me from all my enemies. Just like the man had said to me." Yes, the same one who had given him to me that day on the bed to see.

In the beginning, there was the giver; for this very reason, Steven did quiver. "Even after I'm dead and gone to bed, heaven only knows," the old man yawned and said this to his toes. "Forget the forgotten things, earthen; heathens are those." There he goes, savoring the rose. After noting that there was nothing left here in the form of a question to pose. He was to find out yet more of those, like that same "other man" was still there trampling and walking up and down on his, sorry, I meant to say, "our," on our father's eternal possession. Even then, the very same godly incarnations that he had graciously given. "You know! He gave it unto me on that blessed day when — "When, on which day?"

"On the very day when he was taking those very things away from you and me. But that's okay, I believe, because..." That very same God, oh, my god! It's he or she. It's that same God who is going to avenge me against that man who has proven to me, without a shadow of a doubt remaining, in his right hand. "Or anywhere else left of there," said their best man. Showing it up as proof for me to see that he's my mortal enemy. Yet, it is his gods whom he has given who are going to save me and get me into heaven? Oh yes! I see. This I do believe, though. With all of me, Beau. Because belief is all that I've got left of me, probably. In the meantime, though, look out there, behind the blunt head-bent bow, the beat goes on, on the rows, on the part of that other man, too; look, there he goes. He's out there on the square again, supervising the works of his mighty men. Those who are still on the beat over there, my friend. Beating away on iron and steel. "Must be how biting teeth feel." They're building strong things over there to eat. Such things are meant to keep them secure in their seats. Or in their newfound possession that they would have taken away from me, like roasted meat. Took it from all the other mighty men, too, not you, though, because you're big and strong, bro. So, you must live long, right?

"Right."

Or yet more beating there may be, like. Like how they'll beat you up, all of you. "Or maybe, just some of you and your little pup?" Yes, that is the truth. Beat you up and take what you have left, if any. Or that which you haven't freely given up to him and Emmy yet. Even the very last penny, "and what for?" Had you asked her? To pacify him and to get, like, good, godly gifts, you bet. But he will not be pacified; on such things, we've never lied. Or, for you to go out and get a working man's working job to help him along in the efforts to make and fab... Like, while he's standing by you and watching his team, there, fabricating those fabulous things for him to grab. Made in his factories and research labs, the right thing, yeah man, mad. He wants you to come in and help him build yet more of his very strong things, so designed as to keep him in and you out, no doubt. While he was working, though. You were there sleeping, bro, yes, my brother. Or talking and singing and boasting and grinning. Blogging, vlogging, and giving up information to him, Loggyn. How-to information, even. Now, go on in; the door is open, so go. Go on in and give them to him. Those same kinds of things he uses to build those very strong and beautiful things, to kill. While you're left there with the nothings, still. He, though, continues to build, bro. Yes, building more of his beautiful things, Beau. He built them with materials that he took not from within you, you know? Not from within his borders. You already know that they're those very things that you freely gave unto him in proper order, for you to be able to barter. But he was smarter, so he caused you to give up the very best of everything unto him. In the very act of trading the math that evening, while you were left there with the "nothing," still. The trash remains, too, and things and Ting, then, when he was done with all of the good and best parts of them, the best of those things that you would have given unto him. He sent over the trash, the waste, and the remains. Hazardous waste, even. Where did you want the man to store them, in his own children's playpen? Oh no, not so; that's not how it is going to go to the end, ever. So, he sends it all back to you, as he must. Pack them in and send them over on the Airbus, again. Dump them over on your brain and the heads of your children. Then get you to pay him for dumping them within. Then lie to you yet again, and kill you with it. Then lie to your children after you, and kill them, too, oh sheet. Then blame it all on you, rightly so. Then, those who are left of you, guess what they eventually do? They chose that man, yes, him and his children, (the best). They choose him over you and yours every time. But I guess that's fine. Or should I jest, off-time? No? "No, no jesting behind will soon find what is to be found dead." Go and fund a foundation. Probation, as said. Stop that, I say. Hint-hint. Obey.

2

The Foundation is Funded

"**S**peaking of founding a foundation," said that wise old Larried one, "That's what I'd do if I should win the lottery, too." Yes, I'd do it for all those Lars you know, and their pickney, my child, to get them to grow. Because the children are hungry and getting rather angry, it's now bordering on insanity. "Life of living" for them has lost its quality. Now, go grab yourself a satisfying bite, because this is going to be a very long night, yes, mi star. As you can see, it's going to take somebody who is some sort of visionary. One who will be able to inspire others to join with him and put the proper things in the fireplace for me, so that we may be able to save and reclaim the Larried Lars flame, by redeeming the family name and getting a chance to get in there to salvage the fame of his saving grace.

"What exactly would you do?" he'd asked the old man there, facing off with the screwing tool.

"What would I do? Come sit down here with me, my son. Let me explain it to you and done; let me try to explain to you the tasks." I would set up the foundation, which we spoke about earlier, since you'd asked. So designed to enable my baby brother, and yours, too. If you score well enough to pass, and not just faking it and "jimmying" your way through the class. Like, if you should set the right goals and put them in proper order. That's the proper example for you to set for yourself and your brother. For your son, and other fathers' sons, too. Their sons after them. "True." Go set it up for them to follow and do. Do this to keep the other men from locking the handcuffs onto your Larrie children's hands. "Yeah!" Yeah, man. Swallow it, go on, swallow hard on your spit, if you want. Then go back to the yard, but not just to sit in the weeds farm. Go on, keep on swallowing. That is a good "something" kind of tin to fit you and to wallow in. Yes, man, this is where it all begins. But since you're still sitting here and looking on, with that listening stare on your finger-licking hand. I'm going to continue to show you how much I want you to help us do this thing for them. It's not just for them that we're doing this, but for me and, yes, you too, my Sis. As you can see, the foundation is now up and running, in effect. All the setups are already inset there on the key, you bet. Now, it's time for us to send out the searchlight beams, to go find those boys and bring them in.

"Why, boys?"

"My joys, that's the task." Seriously, though, since you'd asked, why not? Let's take a look at that, shall we? Take another look around you and tell me, what do you see? Then, when you're done, let's sit down here and drop some more chat on your knee, over there. Now, tell me, what is the biggest problem as you see things with the Larrie, lots of them? Which group among them is coming up the back again? No, scratch that "coming up" bit; it's not going to be a good fit. Going on down towards the profit in the pocket of the prophet, yeah! It's the best word for that drift. The Larry Boys, my friend, are sliding down the drains. Someone must do something about those who remain. Like, go save them and those who are coming after them. By doing this one single thing, we might have found a good way to begin.

Yes, the foundation is done, got "get." It's now set up and running, vet. Everything is now (in effect) working towards our progress. So, go out and find the most achieving young man from your learning tree branch. That means, go out there, seek out, and find a deserving young man from within the country where you and your forefathers are from. Fund his journey through university. Even beyond that one, if need be. But all this should come with some conditionality, yes, with the prerequisites all set up already. For example, for a boy to have this joy, his father may not trample; he surely may not miss Troy. "Oh, what is that?"

Had you asked? Let me explain what is meant by miss-troy, my boy. In several aspects of the play, boy, we've framed and worked it so that he, Mister Fatherly Family Manley, man. Mister First-personality, yeah, that one, should not be found missing in action, must be playing the proper role of a father and a man. Living in the home and being an active part of the family is shown. Penning out the family plan, the home life, and the children's lives properly. Providing for the household and the family, preferably.

There was a time, you know, not too long ago, when our Larry women were the ones who were treated so. But those women didn't just leave it sitting there as is and go on pushing up the chair behind those other men there on their axes, playing domino. Still acting up in the seated assets. Oh no, not at all, but… They stood up with an answer and said no to the monster, no more. Now, women's feet are firmly set in the doors over here on the Kingsland shore. Well, I know, I'm sure that there are those of you who will argue that part too, but the time for arguing is far behind you. Behind those other Larry bots, too, even more so as a matter-of-fact stew. It's action time now, and our Larry boys are the losing cow. Come on, man, let's go lend them a hand in saving them.

"What's in it for those fathers?" you'd asked. It's a great question for us to take to task. The father who fits the criteria will be positioning himself to be the recipient of a hefty figure. Like, let's say (just for argument's sake). Let's say, twenty-five thousand dollars' worth of pay. Or the equivalent in gold or other precious metals as sold. This will be his to do whatever he feels. He would have already earned it just by doing the right thing, even out in the fields. The proper things that he would have already done, like when he chose to father his children on the home front. Now. Eat, go on, eat, heat the leftover meal, and go eat it.

Yes. This offer will be good for up to two sons belonging to any such father. No more than two, though, no, my brother. Yeah, man! I'm out of order, I know; I hear you. You're quick to question that queue. Well, let me see if I can tell you why. Or, more to the point, coming out of your high joint, why not? Here's why not. It's because we do not subscribe to the idea of our Larry men going around sowing wild oats in every fertile ground. Nor even sewing all that he can sew in one fertile ground indiscriminately all around the town, no. A Larrie man must plan his family well. He must do whatever is necessary to give each child of his... hell, not just his sons, but all of his children, as you can tell by now. He must give each of them the very best chance at excelling, so they may be able to find their way in the sun where the others are now dwelling. We're not here saying that he cannot have more than two sons. Sure, we are encouraging and advocating for such as the new sounds. But he can have as much as he likes. As for us, though, we'll just take the resources that we've got here to give to his might and go. Taking it along with us to give it to another man and his son. Or his two sons, as the case may be. We'll give them their chance in the sunlight to see, while wishing that other seed-farmer type of man and his family plan nothing but the very best from then on. With the help that the foundation would have just endowed him? He should have no problem achieving the other milestones in his life, as well as in his family life, no problem. None at all.

Note: if the man is going around spreading the seeds far and wide, with the hope that a few of them will manage to make it through the harsh and choking wilderness outside. So that at least some of them may survive. But without his input in their lives, instead of him doing his very best to see that the two sons he has at home are thriving in a proper zone, a set type of setting, and barring none. Then, that man is asking for another kind of sacking. The one that is already coming towards him anyway. We're not here to enable him in this sort of irresponsible and misguided behavior any day. If a man, be he of the Larried clan or any other. If he thinks he's going to ensure his survival by going around dropping off his seeds here, there, and everywhere else, tidal. We're here to remind him that there's no difficulty in having someone else come around and chop off all eighty-seven of his son's heads on one chopping block on the ground, as said. But, if and when that very same brute of an axman should show up on your doorstep to stand. If he finds out that your two sons are among those very same Larrie people back home, who are already marked for death and may be found on the vehicle going down. If he should find out that there's still a lot of value in your two sons, in whom you have invested time, energy, and then some. Like, more resources. Even though those sons of yours were to be found coming home from amongst those other good-for-nothing kinds of people, reclusive. Guess what is likely to be the fate of your two sons, as opposed to all the rest of "them," those gnomes' comb types of other "someone" sons? Go figure it out, and close up that big mouth, before your tongue finishes up with a falling out, of sorts. As for those who are going to argue with you, saying this is unfair and prejudicial, too. Discriminatory, and yet all other kinds of gal friend something sin ting, on which to worry, you know? The fact that we've chosen to focus our attention here on just boys. We did consider that possibility too and tossed it around among us like toys. So, the minute that argument gets to the point where the criteria, as set out in our mission statements from Assyria, are being challenged. Well, not just being challenged, but when it starts facing demands from all corners without qualms, demanding that it be changed to accommodate the other groups, or the individual who is blamed, as is the norm. Based on whatever else may be named, other than these and other such set guidelines? That will be the day when this foundation, the scholarships, as well as every benefit that falls under it. That will be the day when it all comes to an end. Amen. Whatever funds may remain therein afterward shall be forwarded to the entity that shall be named by me and the funders, to go towards... Or, by the executors of my estate, based on the preset criteria, as stated. No more blunders, we're not here to disenfranchise anybody or any group. On the contrary, we desire to uplift and empower people from down there, where they are with you. Yes, that includes Larry's girls, too. Those others whom you are trying to get into this already established group, even. But what you should probably be doing with all that time and energy you have got there to stew and stewing already. It is to go out and form that kind of group for those you can see, who need it, our dear lady. Let me take the opportunity here to say a big "thank you" even now for doing so. That is the purpose and reason for doing this right there. So, go on now, go. Go on out and get started on the task of educating, inspiring, sensitizing, and incentivizing. Meaning, give others something to look forward to, especially those children of yours, and all the rest of the Larrie's crew behind our doors. By doing the right thing, to begin with, and through the front doors of the neat ears of wheat. If we do this for them, then. Even if they did not attain the coveted prize, they will still come out as winners in your eyes. But most importantly, in their own lives.

Any questions? Yes, I see your hand. What's your question, ma'am? (Asking around). You know, my dear! That's a brilliant question right there. She wants to know, "How are we ever going to be able to do this continuously off that little pittance of money?" You know, like, that which was the proceeds of a one-time winning from the lottery phony? The answer to that is this. We use the lottery scenario here just to make a point. (Of beer). But that is never going to be our plan and program for our future developments, jointly. (Look here)! Yeah, man! Go right on. Roll up the joint and take a puff. Good enough for you? Anyway, enough of that phase II, Bey. We have been looking at and taking notice of some things for quite a long time. For many of Larrie's kinds of days, mankind. Looking back over time, we would have noticed that many of our very own Larry folks would have managed to strike it rich, yes, over time. Like, when they were to have gotten fat off the behind-the-scenes schemes of the other beamlines, like this little bit... Then they went out and about, spending all that money on things the other folks sell and tell the hell out of them and him to buy without... and one begins to wonder, why? Why is that? Well, at least some of us did wonder, eyeing his cap, and then. An answer began to take shape in somebody's mind behind ours. Could it be that it's because nobody had ever sat that young man down and told him anything about money and its workings? Or about what is worth having, living for, and spending money on, in this life's lurking? Am I wrong for thinking these sorts of worse things? So, he went out and spent his money on what the other man told him and showed him how to. Something that always seemed to be bending back towards the back pocket of the same "other man," in the scheme of his bandwidth, come on into... Things such as fast cars. Fast cars that he cannot drive fast with her. Not without being made to pay an extra cost, my star. A cost that the same "other man" and his friends would have sat down and made the plans on fast, probably. Plans so designed, it would seem to me, to ensure that he and his friends will always be getting paid off the one-time purchase the "nothing good going on" kind of man had made, when he bought such things for you and them, from him to go rave. Oh no, don't go there, we're not talking about you here. We're talking about that other man over there. The one who just loves and wants to go shopping to hit the post button and share, all the time. Buying pretty nothings for his girlfriends and himself, over there walking the line, nothing spared. Surely that's not you, my dear, right? "Right." But he wants a fast car, as the man had said, and booze on cigars. Expensive wines, too, shook-sisters, and whoreshippers. And many more cutting-edge things to go out and blister, for sure, mister. Well, we're confident that, if we should go out and re-educate and sensitize these very folks, on these facts. They will come around to see that there are other ways to tune the spokes on the bikes, and they might want to join us in our cause. Because, as it now appears to us. One man seemed to think that money is a good tool to use to build things strong and lasting, ill-advised though such thoughts might have been coming off him. No, don't think about it, just wink-wink and go sit. He wants to build things like. Roads, for example, just turn around now and ask him, or look about you if you don't believe in him, and me. There they were, building more roads to come over and deceive me, in yet more fast cars than she'd given me. Cities, too, and country, and all other things pretty and punchy. High-rise buildings and underground infrastructure. Many more such cutting-edge innovation wings and development clusters. All this sort of thing is being done with the technical knowledge that came out of somebody's brain, even yours. But as for the labor and muscle power parts? This is where you and I might "eat a food," again, and fast. Never learning a single thing about the path, up, in the process. Because, again, here's the familiar refrain, such things belong to them, the masters' mistress, and friends. It's for the other men, those others even, yes, you know who they are. Those who were there were giving you those instructions as to what you must do in every detail, for them to get the desired results they want on resale, always. Instructions that you, as a Lar, must follow, and never ask a question. "Just follow instructions," they said to you, and you obeyed the queue. They were born already knowing those things, right? Nobody among them went through any of the trials and errors, overnights, to learn and master anything, no. The other Larry man, though, and his councilors, the very few of our kind who get the itch to go build something, amount to fewer. Guess what he does? He went out and hired that man and his technical know-how. To come over and do the work for him to blow-wow, oh, wow! Then he pledges an eternity to pay him back for it. With the money that he borrows from him, in your pocket (oh sheet!), and continued doing so for a thousand generations after him. Never learning or mastering anything. Other than how to beg, steal, borrow, then die and go to heaven, tomorrow. The very same one that "other man" had built and given to him. Yay, that's the way it's done today, my friends. Those other guys, though, sure, not you, not us either, but them, that's what they do. They do these types of things because they believe that money is good to trample and to go out and buy things, just for example. Things such as clothes, food, chocolate bars, and booze. Blings, and every other glistening kind of "nothings," so. That one went out and built his country and his cities and the roads. The other one seeks out that man's country to go over there and live in his city, carrying the loads. Hastening to go out on those very roads, to go and find himself a job. The job the other one would have fab... So that he can get a little money to grab out of what that "other man" has. So that he would be able to go by the highway, the man had built. Because he had never seen anything quite as big, beautiful, and stealthy. All enticing and inviting. So, he took the invite in and then went out to buy a bike or a car, with the money that he couldn't find to go like, like, to go spar, with, har. So he had to "borr." As in borrow, he borrowed it. Then go up to the top-most heights, to go and fly a kite, like this, and spend the rest of his life in the "owe," you know. Like, just like that logwood stick there on the broad hoe. The one that he already has in his hold and would have used over there before. Then he goes out to drive the borrowed money car down the road and up again. Every day in the sun or the rain. On every stormy night, too, for those none-such remains. None more so than the one in the back of his brain particle. Go on, skip this article if you want. Some truths you and I can't handle, but... Oh, I may be wrong here, so perhaps you can tell me, can we?

Look, the old man is sitting and watching these mad doors four... no wait. He's looking on still and hearing via his listening ear. This is what he's about to see and hear.

"Those squares, my dear, they are everywhere. They can do anything and fix everything to wear."

"Yeah! I know, right after they're done destroying them."

"Oh, no."

"No?"

"No, it wasn't he who'd destroyed them; it was those other wasted waste peoples over there who're swinging off the limb," this he would have sworn before he began to swear at them.

"Oh yeah! Right. Right."

So, now "we" have got to go fix the invasive species of fish in the Great Lakes, yeah. Those Lakers always play to win the stakes, like Vicks. Always victory takers when catering for the Nicks, and now? As to the way it applies to the overfishing of the Atlantic cod?

"Oh my god, child! I know that's bad."

"Yeah! In agreement with you, I nod." But, how about that other thing they were heard saying? Like, that which they say about the stray doggish mentality of others, like somebody, like him. That same one at whom I'm pointing, yes. The same old nitty-gritty who lives out there in the fair city that is oh so pretty. But those are the very ones that can carry her away and marry her off. Then go off on spreading legs as if to viruses on the computer, *"Meh rasp! Ah wah that?"* Now go on, go in and suit her, because. Such a rabid body is those babies, and they should be treated like wild bears over here in the KDs, not like a lady. Now, we've got to do something about overpopulating the pop you lay, Shun.

"Species-extinction prevention, too?"

"Yeah! That should get you some attention, true?"

"No mention, who..."

"I won't, but" who was it that was there speaking wisdom into those noble absurd words like swords? Have you heard? Have you not heard about those same angled mouths that spoke red-sprayed letters before, littering the faces on all the spaces over there on the floor? All this was happening over there on the face of the city's four square. After they were done culling them, yes, the deer, as they were prepared, so to do, so I hear. There were few, if any. Just a few dark-hued circulars were sitting in the chair in that conference room over there when they were doing the planning. Like, when they were deciding to go in and engage the gears, to run over and go run them over to see him, yes, Mister Manning, fair?

"Fair."

So, what do the Lars (same as you are), what do they think of these things? Like, as to how this place will look after the Squares are done with their fixing? Not too perplexing? Worry is vexing, though, no?

"Yes, I guess so."

Lars, as you already know, the way they are. They're not known to be too big on the stinking thinking tartar tar. The after-effects of that which usually come from smoking those expensive cigars. While they're out busily riding away in the fast and shiny cars, even. Starting now, to begin with. However, if Lars should ever one day wake up and begin to be clever, and start to shake up his... "Whatever," and "get up off of that thing," and should (somehow) start doing some pondering, as it applies to these and other such marvelous, wonderworking, miraculous questions, Hingh. I can't help but squander what's left of the wonderful, mighty bumblebee. Or what will be the answer to these nagging floggings now peeping back at him to see? Does he think that, like, for instance? Like, instantaneously after that... after the squared men and their other men of wares are going to go out faster. Put the putting resources on the golfing greens somewhere around there, near the pasture. Their time and energy, too, and such other nonsense- go ask her if you think I'm lying, down there, on the fence, nothing new, and nothing spared. All their other fine things, too, like. Those that are expensive and dare to him and them, not you. After putting it all into the task of culling him and you. Sorry, I meant to say, "Into the tasks of reducing the excess of all other things complex on the population index, of the day," to get to a more manageable and sustainable one... flex, okay? Stop that and listen to me. Thank you. ...only to have him going about as is his customary sin; still shaking his seeding stick all over the plowed and fertile field land at him, and doing nothing about it? Quit.

Back now to those godly personalities of ours, like these. Like, the Gods of the dance, for example. Awesome, those at Savoring the Rose. They're the gods of the dance, I'd supposed. At least, for those whose circumstances cause them to hate and refuse to advance, Sis. Or to worship before them and bow down before their trance sticks. Many were those who had fallen dead at their line-dancing feet. Just from the fear of them eating the meat, and the dread of the dangling beads falling off those biting teeth. Neath, eh, but still, *mek weh dweet*. Yeah, come on, man, let's do this.

Necked there on the breastplate beneath the cheek was where they'd started this practice. Where memories of long-gone tribal ceremonies are often kept on hold for weeks, that's where they saw it, at first. But then again. Those Squares are everywhere, and as things always were with that man, right there. He never takes a break from breaking the faith of everyone. Like people, both small and great, to take from them whatever he wants. No, wait, go grab a plate, and let's dig into some more of this dining sin Ting, I mean, something—"You mean, you don't mind?"

"No, not at all, no problem, man." Because, as everyone already knows, and in remembrance of The Daily Show, Squares never learned how to dance. Like, not nearly as much as how he took to advance. Advancing his purpose and causes unto the stares of others like Lars is. There, I said it. Sit, sit. You mustn't eat your meat standing upright on your feet. Now, let's go out on a beat, as we continue with these- man, this thing sure is sweet. But, like I was saying, they sure would like to, you know, like, learn how to do the dance troop. Lars can teach them a lesson, or two, or three. Now, take a lesson from you and me. Squares were there, floated in on rotten-tempered air, same as it was said to have happened when it was with the waves of the sea. See? Now, look at me and listen. Because, Lars, as you already know how they are, those Lars in particular were far from liking it when strangers stayed beside their backsides, without an invite. Or when they're circling round and about them among the other tribes, peeping inside. They live deep within the woods on the other side. The right side out from the place where, at first, came those restless-eyed, squared, and not-so-gentlemen. That's it right there, my friend. But he'd beaten a path that was still clearly marked, and would have heard of them before he saw what was coming off the hum. Yeah. Humming, as it was to be heard coming from them to fall on him, yes, man, from the most feared Larrie gentlemen. It came hopping into his hearing aid, along with the rest of them, as if to kill them dead. Yes, all of them heard it; the roots rock reggae beating, as already said. Kingsley Square and his trusted rum friends were to follow the rhythm of the beating drums, in. Before they knew what had whacked the hit on him, whack, he would have been down. Whack, yes, they were striking him down, whack. Now look, he's sprawled out on the ground, whack, whack. Out and cold, he went down with a groaning moan like that. Kingsley Square would have hugged the mound. Lars then laid him out squarely on a hardwood bed, almost dead. That's how they carried him in, looking face up at Larry King. But, unlike how it was when they had to whack and wad him. Lars is known to be welcoming. He went out and welcomed him in. So, Larry King would have welcomed him in. That, right there and then, was the beginning of a diplomatic sin. That very evening, after they were over and done with the welcoming of the welcomed, and were to be acquitted of the unexpected respite of wayward sons. They washed him white and feathered the bedpan. Then out in the middle, the Square King was led-leaded ledger. He had to see himself in some semblance of customary Larry ambiance to get them pleasured. The night was young and liberal fun, mixed in with mirth and prime-aged rum. Hands and feet, the squares were numb. Rubbing their hands together with complaints of never having it bled with rum. But, Larried-wise, the facts are well-known as to why (truth be told) it would not go down past Square's deep throat to the Kingsley thrown down. To go walking the path, as it was well known, hung right there where he sat himself down. But then come the rummy drinks from the vessels around. Those cups of old would move around, like, three, four, five, or more feet above the ground. From whence bright brains would have declared the throne, then got thrown, content asunder to parts unknown. Sweat was pouring out liberally. Flowing out all over the square, Kingsley. Falling on boots below his suit atop the seat beneath his peas. Mix in a brew with squared red peas, like when they were seen peeping in the hot pea soup, while watching bubbles boiling over in the fiery smoke coming out of the chicken coop, where we did our chicken-keeping, probably? Well, easy nuh man, why bother me? Don't water the mud, ee. But study the ants, then comes Miss Vomit, oh goddammit. She'd poked a puke-up pannit, yeah man, upon it. Panicking at the truth, yes, that brute was just a youth. Yet, the night was far from becoming mute; there were many more floors left for him to shoot. Come yet more dancing off those Larrie feet, to go and rest in the dust upon his seat. And then. And then. And then. Heh-heh. Look deh. Look, can you not see it? They could no longer stare at his dance. Each squared red face would have soaked his pants while falling flat from the firmness of his stance. That dance did kill the ants, as did the antics. All were (soon afterward) laid out dead there in his pantiac-Ticks. Dust was seen rising on the tops. As Larried feet fell to the fall hard, heavy, and fast. With power balls and speed like a piston blast, as if coming from the boiler room of Kingsley's steamship's ballast. "This is going to cost," he said softly in my ear under his head. But hand me that mask. As of now, Lars has won. Squares, your loss. Oh no, don't do that, you can't stop now. I know, you want to stop, but you shall not be a blow-wow, because. You need to hear what shall be said next. Like a Muta of a shooter would say best, before lighting you up with a burning barracuda, go west. Go on, go in and suit her if she does so. So, again I say, don't go to Chicago to play.

Yeah, man, wordplay is the order of the day here, too.

3

A Cash Crop of Gods

The old man was there looking in at all those gods, and yes, the kings too. He has been around for a long time. Long enough to have been able to see all these and other such happenings. "True." The task has now fallen plumb on him to do the records and tell the stories, such as these:

Gods of the wind: They were great to date, those very gods of the eight. You know them, the eight winds. These four are pushing at your door, and yet four more of them, you want to have those on your safe side, if and when you are seafaring folks lied... Like they were to — "Yes? You mean, they were lying?"

"No, the emphasis here is not on the liars, but the others- we're talking about the seafarers. They were all seafaring men over there. You're doing okay with having the wind at your back. On the backside of the deeps, don't ever stay. Don't let them have to come back upon you, nor up against the glides of morning dew, as they'd done unto those other Rhues.

"Who, unto whom?"

"Them, those over there, look, look at them, I'm a-pointy-fingering at them, those Rhues out there even now, you know, are from among those who did not love, serve, or worship who? Yes. That would be them, as in, those gods, my friends, true?"

"True."

Yes, they were the mighty gods of the wind, but as for them, like those other men! Upon their coming in, the gods would have driven them hard and fiercely; they would have ended up on the pierced, Leigh. You know, like, they were looking steadfastly upon the piercings of the nose, and the earrings they wore in the holes. They were just about to turn around and scamper off, running away from the scene, when they heard the rings ringing in the ears of the pursuers running rings around them. They were trying hard to play it scarce and get away from the doorstep of Lars's own space. Not knowing that the whole region around them belonged to those people most feared for their fierceness. Home to the very people who love and serve those gods. "But for what reason," I asked him, yes, my dad. Because this one "Bad," I could not, and still cannot, ever seem to be able to comprehend a lot. But then again. It was a story of power and still is mighty to shower. Like, like how we'd like to shower you with the wonders of it all. Like, how some men were made able to prosper, up and away from the crawl. While others will not, you know, it's as if they will never prosper. Yes, man, go ask her if you want; she knows everything about that one in the plan, but… The struggle continues, the way it's said by that Raw paw Crawfish paw man, and you, yeah! Based on the facts, there. In his hands to… mouth. It's about those who have the knack for it and those who want it, out. Of knowing where and how to go about getting it, or not knowing a thing to quit. But as for them, those squared ones and friends? They came right on in, riding upon some of those very same winds. Whoring for Ore, and to go raiding the store. Lars saw them coming, way before they landed plumb in there. Yes, look, out there on the shore. He saw them coming and sent for the magicians who would have summoned up the blowers, one, two, three, and four of hers. Spreading the news now, far and wide. This was what I heard. "Go tell it out there on the news, go spread the tidings, tell them how. Tell them all to go and tell the mighty foursome winds to answer the call. Then tell it again, to each one's in-between." That was intended for the other winds, you know. Those who were what they added in between the fours to make up the eight of them. So went the hissing stings off the whistling whim of the whirlwind. She was pointing the fury squarely at them, yes, at all of the squared gentlemen. Those who were coming in with him, too, never knew what had hit a whack upon them, "Ooh!" I know, other than the mightiest of rushing winds. "True." Yes, they came still sailing on in, since that was far better for them than turning their backs to the wind. They made friends with Clem and those other Circular folks around the bend. Good for them, but bad for Clem in the end. But it wasn't for their lack of friends (ships) that they had to go and attend to it, no. Squarely, they were studying the Lars, and that was to cost them dearly for... You know, like, for giving such treasured secrets away, about how they speak to the wind and cause such winds to obey. But then, squares were done only when they were done mutating... You know them, the almighty gods of the rushing wind. He then gave something else in place of them, things that were to leave you dismayed in the face again, and wondering. Oh! How hast thou fallen, oh mighty, godly winds?

...

The reins of Larry King. "You're Right, Zar," said the golden old-end kingly aide, to him, not her. Yes, look, she's the one sitting up there with her friend and watching the two of them, talking. But under his breath upon his bed of death, fit for a king, he said it. "You're right, you are a Lar, he said. But..."

Meanwhile, from over yonder far, look, those two inquisitive were there peeping in through the bar, and eavesdropping on the nook. Here they are. Yes, you can see it all by way of this tiny device that I keep in my car that is so very nice to ride in — "Let me take a look at it." Hop in and let's go for a spin, no, wait, let's hear some more about the great king."

"That's him?"

"Yeah! That would be Elazar," he's the same chief and king who'd looked out and over yonder far. He saw what was about to happen and knew right away, when he saw them, the way they were. They did come in from yonder far, yes, covered up under all that tarter tar. The dusty ash leftover from the cigar, too, was piled up high in the tray registrar, in front of you. They were looking forward to peace and love in *Addie Dan's salle*, filling up with yet more dancers coming in from afar, and yet further ahead of the gar, so it would seem. They were running too, but not in terms of coming to join up with the dream team crew, no. They were running away from their kind of blue-blooded hue. From Kingsley King, that's who. Well, he wasn't king yet. Was just out to steal for a meal and to get whatever he could get. Like, tasty things to eat, and the family's food with meat, you bet. "Look. They're talking again. Look, look at them. He's talking to Edgar, who is talking back at him through the bed bar. Yeah! Look, there they are, the aged king and his... Yes, he's the head bartender, dear, the King's protector and armor-bearer, too."

"That's him, you mean, that's Edgar?"

"Yes, that is Edgar," still standing at the end of the bed bar, where you know who. Or somebody else, perhaps, be it old or new, somebody will be laid out dead in no time, my pops. No matter what, the spread is to be. From a jack to a king under the crown upon his head, tops, you see. Hidden away there and hiding still, from the blue blood he'd caused to bleed, bloody red. The blood that was already spilled, as said, and as you already know, the Larries' thirst was avenged squarely upon Kingsley's thread near his toes, if only for once. But then again... Back to the story as it remains, back to the task of continuing to explain to you how and when it all began, to rein.

It was due to the storm and the darkness that was brought on. They had not seen anything like that before, in their time. Nor has it happened over there again since. They were really worried, troubled over not knowing what to do to kick-start the economy again. "What's going to happen to us?" they asked as if they wanted to know about the trust, along with the things they wanted to have cooked and curried. Then came the other squares, wanting them to share all that they had left over there with them, which wasn't much, to begin with. Furthermore, they weren't even asking, but forcefully taking it from the other's gut, like... Like, taking everything away as if it all belonged to them; they. So, right away, they knew that they would have to leave and go away. To be gone as far from them and their doorway as they could get from the can, airy scars, by tomorrow. If they were planning on living and surviving the day, even in sorrow, so I hear. That's just what they did. They took to the high seas, covered under the darkness of trees, and were greatly aided by the storm that caused the whole situation (the alarm) to begin with. The Larrie King's men were out doing their route. Yeah! He was king at the time, yes, man, that's the truth (of mine). I don't know much about your truth; you might be lying (down) but... The Larried one would have been king long before all of them, yes. Those squared brutes and friends. Yes, those very squared, kingly (fake) friendly messes are who we're focusing our talks on at this address, Sis; yes, that's who we're referring to. It was in the dark of the night, just coming on towards the daylight, when Clem and his men first caught sight of them. Coming in upon the waves and driven by fierce winds. Larry King was ready, yes, ready for the fury. Ready to go bearing down the beer on them like the clouds from heaven's brewery. Clem was young then, and very strong; his men were with him to bear up his arm. They were specially selected from among his mightiest men of war, with their spears and bows in hand, and arrows galore waiting and ready to spar. But there was no need for them to hurry, and scurry away from harr to get back to her again later, because... Those eels were coming in rather slowly. Just a tiny group of sea snakes who'd probably drifted off course and would have been desperate for help to escape, of course. Rather than stealth of sorts, no doubt. So, "Come on in, my friends, come right on in. Come unto me in your tiny sailing thing," said Larry King to them. Well, it was his great son Clem who had said it when, at first, he met them there. It was not to them that he'd said it either. Just there amongst his friends who would have grunted a chuckling laugh with him, under the cedar, so I hear. The squares were scared when the darkness cleared to see that there on the banks of the river was a mighty army, "weird." They would have sworn not to come or go any further, not near enough to try and compare but, but... Oh! Look, they're already too slow, mi likkle bredda. Staring now at the sight of more Lars standing there. With sharp, pointy weapons pointed squarely at them and theirs, dearly. Right there, up under their bearded heads of hair, eerily. The white flag was quickly going up, and trembling legs were even more quickly going to the buck... something, as in the way they were buckling that day.

"Come on in, come into the Larry King's kingly types of welcoming," said Clem, with more chuckles coming out of them, yes, out of the laughing parts of his friends. That's how they were to come into the spheres of the Lars and their kings. They spent a whole solstice span there with them and got a bit too comfortable under their shins. But then. The day was to come again when other squares were to come and pass by them, coming in from the cold with tidings, like gold. Telling them that the storm had passed, and the warring skid had ended. The time is now ripe for squares to leave the lands of the Lars where they had landed, to be gone again to their place in the rain, far and backhanded. But that wasn't the way the story would have ended, because... Everybody knows it by far; they never stop when it comes to the war.

Lars are Lars and squares are squares, yes, but... While they sojourned there on the land, those squares were in command. They would have managed to build up strong ties with the Lars over there. Yeah! So, I hear. On that side, the relationships would have carried on over periods that were long and wide as branded hardware, up until the time of Kingsley King II. By then, though, as you already know this truth, the relationship between all those squared and shapely folks within their borders would have softened. They were becoming friends and brothers again and met up with each other often. Not that it did put a taw of any sort on the "great" relationship of hearts between Lars and their newfound friends. At least, not as visibly as it was to come across to them easily, by then. But everybody knows that blood is thicker than milk. It's smoother and stronger than even a gar... net silk. Most definitely, thicker than a palm-full of Larry's drinking water from over on their side of the pasture, and mixing it in with the silt. No, not now, wait until after, you know? Like — "You mean like, like, to get into the laughter that I'm already after?"

"Yes, that's the correct answer. Now, move along, faster," because… Look, those wandering squares and the Kingsley Kings of theirs are so tight now that not even a light out of a very dark night can seem to get in between them. Certainly, not such a weird thing as a Larrie King to wean them. However, they had sworn to remain the very best of friends, even to the journey's end. That was then, but this is now, and as you and everyone else already know, some men are like cows; they never go, no matter how hard one may drive them. There are some others of those kinds over here, too, others who are just like them, and you. "Moo!" The same thing can be said to be true with them, like, they're those who were found to be in need, yes, of surgical lenses like these, if nothing else. They can't ever seem to see very far in front of them. Yeah, that would have been as meanly meant as it was when it was seen happening to him and them; that same Elazar and his friends, yeah man, like… the said Larry King and his sunny, suntanned children. So I heard them say, "Don't shoot this messenger, okay?" So says all of them over by the bay. "But are they?"

"Not really, if you ask me." he was not one such a man. To be fair to him, he wasn't always that way, as weak and sickly as he is today, c'mon. He was known to do and say powerful, lasting things to obey. Like, valuable things for his people to pursue, and working, wonderfully poetic words for them to obey, and you? His father before him, too. Like, that same Clem, that's who. Yes, that would have been him. He was not one of those men like the rest of them. But as for the squared king and friends, one could have sworn scared that he was upended. Offended to be named among those over there as friends did, when it all was to come undone and end… dead. Like, when all the "other types" were to find themselves pushed out and forced from there and gone, near the end. "Ding." But he was not to be given the chance to choose for himself whether to stay or to go with them in, or out. Insults like those are never to be left unattended, no mi scout.

This was the cause of what had happened. Because of the friendships that were established between those two (they were long-established).

They were made able to cross the great divide going to and from, like this. But that squared one, as you already know the song of the man. He doesn't play fair, and most definitely, he doesn't ever go slow. At least, not when it comes time to step down hard on the other guy's toe. So, by the time the Lars had gotten around to looking back in the cars. The squares were filling up all of the spaces over there in their backyard. In the back seats, even, and majoring in the bars. Those places were the most chosen, as seen via the squared eyes on their face, my cousin, to be fair, and coming to them from afar. He was even seen playing the role of boss over King Elazar's ass... as... assuming things that he should not have been. I know, sometimes one has got to take bad things for a laugh (yeah! even with him) and then go. Even though the head squares and their Kingsley Square weren't there. Do you hear what I hear? He was not there, but a hundred years from this day, mark my words and re-member it to match-make her go and face it up with the replay. There will be squares and those Kings of theirs sitting in the chair of King Elazar. By then, King Elazar will only be remembered as the great, long-time king of the mighty Circulars. Place a bet on it and then go spar, the dice with ours, even. Because everywhere his feet trod upon another man's ground, dead tag, in those times. That's what he was doing: thiev-ing. He was claiming it as his very own, not mine. But there was one Lar who knew them from afar; he was different from the rest of the Lars by a scar. He knew enough to have known that he did not know a thing or even two. Or twenty-three trees, go on out and count them off for me, please, oh no, wait a minute, don't bother with it, my friend, not while I'm in it, with these. Let's just carry on with the other everlasting "ever-after offerings off the sheet." So, he'd proposed it there and then within his knees, to go out and learn, and to copy the already established norms, see? "Yes." To try and learn whatever he could earn, or how to return what he could not burn, and store it in a city called Hearne. He did learn some things on the road coming in, though. But then?

Elazar is now old and waiting to hear the bell toll. "What profit is there in gaining the golden girl, and then losing the real prize, the world?" He was heard asking this of the young prince's fish, while looking in through the aquarium glasses, ish, via the lens of what was a gift of offering, as was given to him by the squares at one of their passages. This was intended to be seen as a sign to him of what wonderful things were being done over there in their hallowed spheres. Those were the kinds of things that could easily be done amongst them, too, he'd said. For the benefit of him and his kind over here, "his crew," yes, mi bred. If only they were to become friends and great allies, riding on the squared kings' vehicles beside his backside, and mounting upon the heights, like a kite. But that would have happened only after he had heard about his son's attested exploits, reaching out for a Square offspring to be his wife. That was when he spoke through the glass of the aquarium that night and wondered out loud. "What is it that has now befallen, my son?" He wondered and asked in concern for him — "*Wait, mi just accom...*" "I know, take a seat below." He was red hot there under the collar and blue in the face, enraged at the general's pronouncements that he'd made, while he was grazing in the grass yard, and not laughing too hard at the intentions within his beating-off chords. He intended to go take it to them, like, to go over and do them in. Now that the old king is just about gone, and the young are in, or soon it will begin. The princess, too, was young, alright. "True." But the power belonged to her over there by rights, not you. Clemson was about to inherit the throne from his father, Elazar, in another hour or shorter, as short as the little pigmy that you are. Okay, yes, mi Breda, I know, you're a lot smarter than har... However, the general has the right, at least at this stage in the young prince's life. She wasn't the king's first choice to become the prince's wife.

"But, but, but this is my life," Clemson the prince would have advised the advisor who was an outsider to his inner circle provider. But was inserted in, to be there, mixing and mingling with him. "Apparently," as was heard said by somebody, "upon the wishes of his father, the king, the Larry King," who was (coincidentally) to be going the way of the burial ceremony, shortly! Or was it? Was it the king who had sent the outsider in? Oh, sheet. The correct answer to that question seems to be still somewhere out there and blowing in the wind. He'd fallen hard for her sugar chord, even though she was not a super Lar like these over here in the yard, but she came right on in, riding high upon the tributes-paying train, to pay respect to the dying King again, but then. She ran squarely into sweet Clem, no, not that Clem, but Clemson, my friend, and we don't want you to confuse the two of them, the Clems. That is why we don't want you to be heard calling them here by their common names over there. Anyhow, beware. It's not like it hadn't happened there before; everyone there knew the score as to how that was frowned upon, the door. But the young prince was not fazed. "After all," he said, "these are modern days. Things have changed from the old depravity, and glory now lies up ahead of the gaze." The king would have relented to sin and allowed changes to begin. Now, everywhere around the kingdom throne, there is... Look, look at it, see what I mean. There is joy and laughter everywhere. Replacing frown and fear, after the gears of Mae Ray's and Marsha's turn at sharing the ginger beer. You know, like, after the afternoon's dream team was done with having their time, spraying the sayings all over the platter they had given him, and into the sorrel wine. Prophesying what is going to happen next, yes, no denying anything, yet. Look, they're there even now, making predictions as to what will soon be happening around this modern-day kingdom's throne to blow-wow. To this particular one, too. Look, look at the cow who's just about to sit down on the moon, in that nook. "Yes, the one who..." "Moo." Well, the joy and laughter were to be heard everywhere, but... Tough luck for somebody's but, but, but now, please. Shut up and go put the button in the buttonholes on these.

But really, though, who was it? Who could that garment fit? Something rotten was just about to happen at the mixed-up marriage in the coffin, sticks, sorry, I meant to say, besides the coffin, okay? Look, look out there where it lay. But how could Lars not have known that far, to have mistaken the fact that some of them were merely clowns, not stars?

"Acting the parts unknown with her, right?"

"Yes, Mister, you're bright. For the greater good of a squared house and home."

"In the hood?"

"Maybe, but that's not good, so..." This is how it was said to go, by the same person who'd told me so. Alright?

Once upon one of those times, he began to look out over the waters again and was to find that he, and all of his kind, had fallen like me. Yes, just like all of the Lars' den, he too had fallen far behind them, for a farthing (can't see). So, that was when it started to happen again. He knew right there and then that he would have to go out and spend the necessary time. Over time, too, if he were to catch up in line with the rest of mankind, such as you. So, he went out with his fishing gear, and he was about to make some wrong calls in these over there, yes indeed. The house of Clemson, too, would have ended up making the league with this Kingsley, true. Or more like, with someone in his line, dimly.

"But, but who..."

"How would I know, you...?" His wrong call was about to come calling, in some faraway place at the far ends of the seas. A place called something like the Waist in Deeds. Yes, indeed.

Meanwhile, he was there, yonder far; he was not a Lar. Surely not like those round deads, and the Circulars, but he was still sitting up there on his rocking chair. But with nothing left to spare, it was all gone by the end of the storm that year. The snowstorm had kept him in, way up there. That was the way of the squares over there, to sit and rock on, like, baby rock on. As they would dance and party all night long. Yet, to be fair, it wasn't all happening just there, and there only. It was the time of the kings. There were very many of them on either side of the dens. Over there were the squares and their fair kings, but on that other side over there — "Oh no, stop pointing over here, not here. It has never been here, Sir, I swear, but there, over there."

He may complain, yes, but... Just like squares, Lars and their kings were also fair. Until they ran into each other and started studying one another there, well, one was studying the other. In truth, only one of them was, like, studying. As for the other? He was being studied, but not knowing a thing about these, like it is the custom with things when it comes to him and his buddies, oh please. With all of them, even those rounded circular gentlemen never bothered to study "nuttn." I mean, anything going on over there that's worth knowing, my friends? Ask them again and see what answer the old man has left under his pen.

Meanwhile, while these things were happening, even as they were happening. Somebody was found in his room grumbling. Wondering hard at some other things that were going on around him. Then came his rumbling sound in, "Where did my little piece of the peace go?" He hissed at the beast, oh, but it was to cease. "No." Yes, because the malicious code of Ray had saturated and increased over the day. A violent stream of lights pierced through the night, and the sound of silence was to become a thing of violence.

"Will... hey, William, tell me, will... will this be the end of innocence for them?"

"Might well be, my friend, look." Clem is gone, and Elazar, too, has just moved on. He fought it well and moved on. He was a really strong King, and he beat the brute back, although he was an old man and was beaten to the bones within; smacked. Go on, hurry on over yonder, and ask him if you want. Before he could have chased them away, though, they were to start noticing the latter end of him and all those Larrie men.

"Oh no!"

"Oh yes," he now calls them friends again. Yeah, that would be Clemson and his men. They were to make leagues with him; invitations get sent to visit the visitors, and the reverse of that is the next verse. They became close too, much too close for the comfort with which Clem and Elazar were comforted by you and your walking shoe. Until the truth of Kingsley's boot was to walk the route. Now, all that once belonged to Clem is to become Kingsley's loot. But now that Elazar is gone, his young son Clemson is in command. His grandson, really, Clemson is now in command in the kingdom, living royally, and a square princess sits on his right hand. The right-hand of royalty, some might say to me, about the man. What's the plan? What is going to become of them, everyone?

4

The Beckoning Calls of Kings

Hear ye, hear! Listen to the beckoning calls of those kings, over there: Pictures hanging on palace walls. Warhorses, too, were neighing in the stalls. It's a picture-perfect portrait ordained to tell the story, yet. Of all those kings were about to get, from the rejects, as well as other hidden secrets of that square, Kingsley-King's set. All their stories are enthralled in the beckoning calls to their glories after all. This began to change upon other happenings down the lane, such as were to come floating in just after the forming of the dark morning, in the rain. That thing that was about to come floating in upon them next, without a warning. Like, when the skies were found covered in volcanic ash. When everyone there thought that it was the end for them and that everything they had would have gotten mashed. Like, a lot of stash and pork barrel of potatoes. "Oh gosh!" But then, the skies clear up again, the gods would have fallen "the former rain". The meadows were lush with green again. Birds sing, and clean water springs to life in the springs, for them. But there was a lot more lacking than that left locked up within. The land was ravaged, almost consumed. "In six months from now, there could be many things here to harvest the moon," said Kingsley to all the rest of the goons. Of course, he wasn't King yet, but that (renewal) would depend on how many "seeds" they might have left in the basket on the head of the new gal, and on how much strength might yet remain in the might of the squares' mighty men, and to be found still hanging about their necks. There was a problem and only one way to solve it. They must first build up their strength, which they did. But upon the backside of the other kids, those living right there on the homely blocks of his, yes, those kids. Even their very own stacks are all-inclusive. They were all Kingsley, only separated by their number in line, dimly. Kingsley1 would have happened to become king just after the end of the fast, which was brought on by way of the darkening darkness, Mass Vin. If you had bothered to ask him, he would have told you everything. They didn't know what the cause of it was. Not at first glance, mi cous. They thought it was a curse from the gods of the curse. Accompanied by way of their nurse, the church. "But of course." What it was, in reality, was drifting lava dust and smoke, literally. The direct aftereffects of a volcanic eruption several thousand miles away, beyond the valley, across the ocean's bay. It was one of the biggest such events ever to have happened in their human monetary history. Well, that, according to his story, as it was given to me. "Or was... wasn't it mine?"

"Same sign, stories are they, all the time." The dust was next to come riding in upon them. Carried along by way of the winds that were blowing things to cover the sun's face from viewing the disgrace around them. As such things were to be seen happening over there, in that place, starting from within. Other than for the immediate results of folks stumbling around in sobbing sulks, while walking around in darkness before, unknown, and witnessing such dreadful results, all around the town. The worst was still in the waiting room and hastening to come. Yes, it was right over there in that tiny room up ahead. Can you not see the bed? Answer up, man, don't just sit there nodding your head; we're on the radio, not Television. Two to three years after the initial spread of the eruption's dread. It was to stay, yeah! That same one, along with the suffering in the aftermath of the volcano that had erupted. It was to come spreading in for long, before it was gone, again. Yes, it came in from way over there that year. Or did it? Maybe not, but it was the only thing that they could imagine after the act of that time. Like, when it was first made known to the kind folks in that region of the toe, you know? Not in that neck of the woods this time, but the toe.

"Why, though, why do you call it that, the toe?"

"Because it was about to become a world-class kind of dragging tow since you'd asked me to tell you all about it, and how it came to be so." Two, going on three years later, the real effect started hitting them greater and more deeply, around the answering parts of your asked favors. I mean, theirs, not yours. Right there at the home border. Yes, right up there where they lived at the time. "Too out of order." Because the sun had not come shining through upon the squared lands fair and blue for all that time. Blue-blooded, though it was, and very well-studied, too, yes, it was the home of their beloved, filled with bugs. "Who?" "You." Before the waters got all muddied under them, the food stock stack pile was to suffer the spoiling. Then, they began to get hungry again, and Wandering was beginning to befriend the Bungie thing, yes, their friend. Wink-wink at him. That was when he was heard wondering loudly at the sink, near the sea. He was wondering what it all meant, "For me," and from whence the food would come, to fade out hungry and bring us back the lump sum. "It had better come, though, and quickly." So said he, to nobody in particular, Leigh. Not long afterward, blood would have been spilling over their swords. The man over here had to hit hard at that one over there, in the yard.

"Oh, Lord!"

"Yes, each one targeting the other one who was to be found unwilling with his giving hand and not giving up a portion of his belly-filling to others for their living, fei nyam. Or all of it. To leave him with nothing but himself and the "nilling" to go bawl out and kick. It happened very quickly. So quickly that the man was forced to become fit, fit, fit, Leigh, and waxed. To be able to make a number-one hit on the charts by hitting the "fixing" flex and to be found there, fitting it into the mix, yes. As such, things were to be seen coming down to the meet-up and rendering it tender in the blender, coming in next. So, this man over here was forced to fall upon that one over there, and he did "nilled" him. Just to take what was in the pot, the other man was chilling. If the willing ones were to become unwilling? He takes it from them, too, to go toward his healing.

"Or towards his effort at joying up his family's feelings, right?"

"True, I guess, yes—"...only the strongest from among them was going to be standing best, in the end. Or to still be found there, standing up for the longest. Of the run that is, and to be found still standing there, at the end of the quiz. Kingsley was one such friend; mighty were the flames of his fame. He went out and about over there, making for himself a name. But then, the sun came out from under the dusty spout and started shining again, against the shouts. The crops even prospered in the ever after Ward, but...

But Kingsley had tasted the nectar, the sumptuous sweetness of the spoils of war. Can't just go back now and stop the car. "I can't go back and turn things around after getting this far," said Mr. Mister. The man was forced to fight the war, all because of the fall of the star. Or was it? That, as you already know, wasn't so. But that sort of talk was all that they could pass off before they'd gotten to the truth and found out that it was coming off the volcano, yes. It was volcanic tar. But as for Kingsley King? From then on in, they're not doing anything by him if they are not to be seen doing war things, along with him.

"And, and, wasn't the decision coming from among the rest of them?"

"Yes, they were all hastening on in for the taking. Partaking in the raiding, and scoring a share in all of the spoils, and yes. After the ash mess? They got together and crowned Kingsley much better. Even the very best, the best warrior that they would have had yet. They then went out and about and weren't the proud men stout? Yes, they were." After that, they would have gone further in, taken a strong-arm hold upon him, and crowned him king. Kingsley King, the very 1st. That was because, as things were turning out? He was being seen as the best thing for them. The rest, as they say, is his story. No, not mine, no glory for me divine. Okay! I hear what you say. I'm cutting it out, okay?

"Note from the author," Just a note of thanks to you for choosing to read my book and sticking with it to this point. You must have liked it a lot. "Oin't." At this point, I want to ask you, my reader, and my friends, to take a minute or two to post a review of the book on the sales pages at Amazon and any other such sales pages, then move on. Now go. This small gesture is so very much appreciated. And don't keep it to yourself, as they did; be sure to share the love; tell someone. Thank you.

5

Happening on the Other Side

Meanwhile, other things were happening somewhere down the aisles. While the squared men over there tried, things were also happening on this side. No, not that far a glide in to reach over on the larried Lars' tide in. At least, not yet. It was happening somewhere over there, though. Somewhere over the rainbow, where there had earlier landed some other square toes. Squares who, themselves, had become aware that life was fair, very fair indeed, for those who will dare to go faring, and to act on these. So, they would have dared and disappeared from over there alongside those other squares who were akin to them. They would remain the very best of friends, too, even to the journey's end. "True." But this was happening in the dawning part of their waking-up morning. There would still be many storms to be forming, "and sunny days for us…" meaning, them, "to be warming." So they warned the company doing the farming. Before there should come the calm, and yearly ears of corn.

Speaking of corn, this is the norm. To be reapers of corn, there need to be keepers of barns on fertile farms. Now, this is where visionary and shapely bearded men like these get the stem cells called stamina, oh please. "I'm coming right on over," said Bungie and his unfriendly soldier, "somebody" kinds of people, things. Yes, his brothers and friends were creeping in. You know them, not really his friends, as they pretend, but his followers. They were following him for the allowance they were allowed, and all the other things too, for crying out loud. Coming to them from the little brother to whom they all bowed. They were more than just a brotherly crew. Well, it wasn't all of them who were there doing the saying; Bungie did the saying and the sending parts. But it was his brothers and the others who were amended to be able to pay him the smarts. You know, like, by paying the necessary attention to him and obeying... the boss. Surprisingly, they did, okay? They obeyed and went in. Inside the house, they went to see him, and then into the ships and out on the sea, to win, yes, that would be us. Trying to spy out and see whatever there was to be seen. "Seen?" "Yeah, man!" That was how they found and brought back the tea. But then, in comes the p, as in people. Including him in the vehicle. Yes, him too, the Larry King, Boo-boo, well, not the king. He didn't come in at that time, not yet. He did get on board the sailing shelf, however, and would have enabled them to go in and sell themselves to whoever. As in, his people belt, which was not too clever, but... Everybody was doing the selling thing in those same days. Hell, even those who were buying were doing so just to try out their arm at selling things. To go off bumping up the golden pot and welling themselves off that, in some ways. Yes, getting richer off the wealth-swelling sin, Mister. That was how it all got started. But then, Kingsley would have wanted, you know, like, he wanted in on it. He wanted to reap what he'd previously planted and quit. But he would have been reaping it off what Bungie would have sailed the seas in ships to go over and get them watered, with. That was when the king sent messengers in; those same men that were sent in to fetch the Bungie fellow, thing, "and bring him in." Yeah, that was what he said to them, and they brought him in to stand before the king. Yes, he, the said Kingsley King in command, and a new way would have been born. But then again, back to those gods of mine, those that you're now leaning on, like, Gods of the dead: Those who were never really dead. "They'd just moved on up in the featherbed," so they said, and were to flee and fled out of there. Then go much further along the road ahead, towards Vanity Fair. Trying to fare much better with more power and strength, I hear. To enable them to serve those who love and worship them. But then, Squares would have hopped right on in and all over them, yeah man! Right there and then. Well, you know him; that square-faced man was going everywhere in those times. But it wasn't for the lack of fear that those squares were there watching the dollar whine. He was trying but could not conceal his lying... something sin Ting, no. He was shaking down there, you know? Somewhere down below the spare-legged tare, above the toes. The limb that was usually hanging off the upper half of him, yes, there. Just above where it overshadowed the calf... Oh no, not the cow in the "pass..." where it was pastured and eating grass. Like, where it's called up and often barbed-wired in and cordoned off, no, but he was trying his very best to get up and walk away from the very place where they were to barely let him say "Lay! Lay, lay off." They did, laid them off, and left him with just enough breathing breath in the bagpipe-like breath-taking chest of drawers to say it. Piped in for the watering request and to stay for a layaway on the layby. Like, as in, them granting him his request to let him and his men stay in there for the night and not hang him on the thing they were hanging around for. "Yeah! Right." In there, and to stay on the outer course, and then get off their coast by morn, to be gone away from where he had swayed off balance, all the while, though, not even sparing a smile, no. The thing that was known to clown the tumbling down of his fierce wrath. That thing often comes from the tried, tested, and proven men of the cloth, on their behalf. Those from over there on the other side of the great divide. But they were to hop a spot on the truck for a ride over and to get back in there before he and the rest of them were to get sent somewhere. Yeah, Lars was going to send all intruders there off to the other-sided sphere, weakened and spent, by the weekend, I hear. Like, to go back over there, eventually. So, the squares were buoyed, but they were sort of nearly destroyed. "Shuts!" And, and what for, you'd asked her? For having taken one wrong turn on the way up, upon the quest to come into the deaders' hut. They would have known right away, though, that they would not... You know, like, they would not want to stay too long a time in the region, and among this kind. That would have happened when squares looked up at what there was to be. They didn't like the eyes that they'd turned around to see. Or more like, the place where eyes used to be. Nor were they amused by the more than enough bone-headed bones of jewelry, as worn there, upon those Lars's bodies, as some sort of enhancement or mechanical beauty. Yes, honed and very well-toned were those bodies, in what was the custom over there, at the Lars territorial fair, yes. It was the customary way over there for the people to worship and wear... yeah, I swear. They wore the boned remains of departed ancestors, as in the skin and upon the vein. No *jesting sinting* something things. Yeah, man, *yardman sin ting,* again, you know. Like, like teeth and small bits of sweet toe-toes that were to meet up with the defeat of the foes. They shall all come to the fall at the feet of those who had lived very long and notable lives, but then came the rut, and now?

"I'm out?"

"No, wait a minute more, man, this little bit is very important to the score, Ram, so..."

"Yes, you're right, I guess, so..."

As for those Larry men, like the greatest and chiefest of the elders, even those who aspire to be future leaders. Just as much, too, were the youths who wanted to live long enough and to get to be elders, like you. What do they do? They would wear the bone on the roundups, while out and about doing the round-up, near the huts. The boneheads of the elders who are dead were worn right there on the top of the fire-head, as such things were known over there, and as already said. On the heads of those who were slated to become the head ones in the leadership races of their kindred. Squares would have seen this when they'd wandered in unfit. Unprepared was he, yes, the King, Kingsley, and was scared stiff out of his barbed, bearded wit, Leigh. Quickly, he whispered and said what he wanted to say to the snitch, me. He wanted to disappear, but he never got anywhere near it. He didn't get as far as where he really should have veered. "Oh sheet!" Like, to go away, ever to stay. But as everyone already knows, that squared thing: that never goes away thing, never did; he never goes. At least not far enough. Like, into forever, Mutt, yes, Wilmot, but over there? Look.

They were there at the meeting in the square, in an airtight room somewhere. Discussing boom for themselves, but gloom and his friend doom for the other men, bereft of his wealth. Chiefly, doom for the circular den, with my help, even.

"I want all of it," he was heard to have dit when he said it, and they laughed. They all laughed at this, but as for him. He wasn't laughing, not at all. He was as serious as he could have ever been, Paul. But they couldn't see any of it along with him then. Not until they were to see themselves among them, you know? Like, sitting at round tables among those other men. As well as finally getting around to seeing the vision of themselves fitting in permanently, somewhere in there. In their respective place among those other men over there, like, like, decades later. Centuries, even, for the offspring of some of those roaming crop takers. That, though, all of that stalking and sidetracking, would have started on that very evening when he would have claimed all of it for himself, and them, those other thieving... something. From Larry, forefather king of Clem, and Elazar, and Clemson, and... "Yes, from all those others around and about him." From the whole circular mess, Hingh. He claimed it for all of them, and his children's mouths were moving... in. But for the most part, all of that claiming? It was still hidden from the hearts of the brainless whim. Like, like, from the hearts of all of those who had already been claimed by him. Like, from those circular lame ones, for instance. Just for example, my friends. All that was left for Kingsley to do was to follow through, go out, and stake the claims upon what he had claimed from you. Yes, from me, too, and them, and to make it known unto them and us that, although they, I mean, we. Although we did not know it yet? Though we didn't know how things were about to go.

"Where, west?"

"Probably." But you'll do best if you follow me. Because, in no time at all, everyone will come to know that their time had come, and that time, as it was, was to go. As for them, though, as for those Larrie gentlemen, and how it pertains to their children in the future from then on. As all of it would apply to them, and what was left hanging off their arms? They were to become nothing more than bigger beggars, staring away from the header, while looking forward to the never-ending nether ends of them, and their beggarly begging children. But they didn't know that either. Just a teaser, bar, of course. That was then, though; this is now. Go.

6

The Sharing Night of the Knights

They were all there, splitting up the spoils and sharing the shares. Like, such gear as the sifting of the tares, as well as the wheat, and all the treasures they would have taken from thieves. The convergence of conscience was to meet up there, too, and the unconscionable was made able by, guess who? As for the unconscious, though, no, he didn't bother to show. Look, there they are, gathering the assembled and trying to assemble themselves in the car, becoming more orderly to become as strong as you are, and even stronger than Har, I mean, her. But the assembly was soon disassembled and dismantled asunder. All because of the antics of some of the assembled Leighs, who will not be assembled with ease. Nor do they want Ted to ever be seen with anybody else except among these, like... Like, with thieves just like themselves, please, probably. Or with someone else who is more like themselves? Maybe, just maybe, why bother me? But they would eventually be assembled with some other "Someones," no matter what is to be the outcome qualms. Especially if and when it may become convenient for this one to be with the other man. Even if just to suit and satisfy his circumstances. They were gathered there in the square.

"Oh, you mean... wasn't it in a square concept of a Kingsley room somewhere?"

"One way or the other, they were there amongst the brothers, trying to gather themselves together, to become stronger for much longer." But over yonder, look, across the table by way of a pointy finger. That white-bearded one would have wondered. He was wondering if this would turn out to be remembered as a blunder. Yes, man. He was there wondering this out as loud as rolling thunder, and yet more wonderful wanderings were walking in between the other brothering, as he wondered yet more, at the younger... Wandering around the pit and wondering if his interest, just like all the other interests that he would have accrued to himself, would have managed to possess. All by way of his smarts, and by incest, sorry, I meant to say, "invest." He had invested much in himself and his commonwealth, you know. For all the common poverty that he would have sold, and gone. Yes, man, sold them a six for a nine every time. Deadly poison, too, he would have sold and to the others dealt (a crime) upon the eye scabs of the blind, while taking away the wealth that was thine. "Will it? Huh!" He was heard to have wondered and spat. (Spit). "Will it all be taken away and squandered under the watchful eyelids of the governors, who are out there selling reparation powder, even now? Will their ways and what they're saying catch fire and backfire on us to land us in a wayward place? Like, in a place and a sit you Haitian, where all that we now have will be taken away and given over to others like them, they, like they are? I mean like, like, you? Will it all be given over to you, and you, and him, that one over there too, and not us, but to, to, to them?" There he goes, pointing the finger ring around the room in rows, pointing them all out, over the memorandum, and the notes. Those who'd been sitting there all these years, comfy in knowing that they were counted amongst the squares. Even though everybody there knew that they were really two or three basis points on the circular side of the chairs. Never was an issue before, but now, all of a sudden, they are. If only in the eyes of one as scared as you at the bar. They would have fidgeted away from the meeting of the assembly. So, even though the squares were there, and the cubes, too, I was not there, nor were you. I'm willing to give two bits or bet a dime on it.

"On what?"

"On that, the fact that you were not, like, you were not there." You're not a square, let alone a cube. Every cube is a square, even when cuboids are packed together in a long tube that's square. But not the reverse side of that, like... Like, where cubes should disappear into becoming a square, no. Repairs would be fair, for that said, Square. A rectangle won't ever have to ramble along, arguing about the mishandling that he was handed by the man. Nor will he be humbled and start to grumble about the gift. He was wondering if it was a mistake that he should have stumbled upon it, and found himself a place there amongst them to sit. Like, when he was to be found bundled up with the rest of them there. "Oh sheets! No," he said, "this isn't fair." So, two are the few that will do, if they are Triangles, like you. Though they tend to fit in better whenever they assemble this one with the others. A line will gather itself with others of its kind, preferably with many others such as thine, so he'll be able to get in every time, even in a straight line. But there are those "Others," like others who are badder. Well, of course, in their bladder, perhaps. Well, of course, they were bad. Yes, man, they were badly designed from the opening line of their hopping in time.

"How so?"

"You mean, you don't know? Because they can never seem to be able to stand on their own upon a hill sloped down the mine. "No?" No, nor can they ever be trusted to walk and fine... Like, fine-tune a straight line." They just seemed to be able to roll downhill and tumble and stumble until... and that is all. All the time, and all around the ground. For no lack of rolling around, and a generous, liberal dusting of black and varied shades of brown. Outside and around, yes, outcasts they are and are known. When seen from afar, they are, yeah, man! You know them; they're the mighty circulars, my friends. Circulars will never fit in, so it would seem, except when they're to be seen fitting things into the kitchen beam, perhaps. In the sink, too. While sinking somewhere over there, beyond the blue. Somewhere in the spheres of the squares, mostly true. In the bars serving beers, too. Or on a stage, dancing, singing, and making a mocking fool out of fooling around with something. Not someone, though, not anyone but themselves, Bro. Hanging onto the shelves, sometimes. Dangling off the walls and stalls, at other times.

Stalling the car from the start, and doing yet more walking, talking, telling, and... and — "And what, entertaining?"

"Yes, but I don't like it that much whenever you butt in like that, night and day, Hing."

"Okay, I won't, I, I'll try not to do it anymore, okay?"

"Thanks." Like I was saying, entertaining the idea that he, they, all of them, and me. They... I mean, we. We like to think and say that we've arrived, squarely now, on the other side, yes. "Squares are mixing in," they were to have lied. Mingling, too, and playing on par with Lars. Progress so far, yeah, my star. Prosperity isn't too far.

7

Chimes of the Times

Listen, there go those chimes again, chimes of the changing times, my friend, waking the old man from his sleep chamber where he was lying... down, yes. In the beginning, the squares were there, warring against themselves from that morning on the square. It started immediately after the dark leftover nightly disaster, up there. "It was like tribal war, more like, survival for — "For what?"

"For this, and that, because man needs food to stay fat and staying alive, staying alive, staying alive... by the fireside with his eyes peeping in on the boiling pot." So, for this cause, they had to strive, trying to find the next little morsel to get stuffed into the next leather parcel, to stay alive. So, they tussled; hardheads were breaking bottles. But then the sun came shining out again, and warring families became the best family friends; it could have been the end of innocence for all of them over on the foe's falls. Or worse, even, the end for all of them in the cow stall, or for the whole sum of them put together to crawl. But as for you, and him, like, King Larry, too? Yes, look at him. He even slid over backward and fell over the falls, with you. But war fever was still in their veins — "Leave her." Spells death and destruction on the other insane giver. The lust was to come bursting with righteous religious crosses, trusting. Then they crossed over the continent's pastures, and that was when Kingsley was crowned king faster, by men who were warring with him mere moments earlier, even, no jesting. But that was then, that was before the sun came shining out again. Now it's still not okay, but as for some of them there, like, as for him, that very same one even, it's raining mainly hay, as it was in the hay day.

Kingsley would have heard of it; he heard about the magic that Bungie would have nicked. He'd received words that the other squares over there were whoring for profit, and finding plenty and to spare of it. He knew right away that this was his big hit, yes. He was back at the place where he could go out and get back all the bakes. "Wow!" You know, that bundle of money that he had at one point but would have lost, yes? "Yes, it aches," because such were numbered among the things that were to become wasted waste in the frost pit. He would have lost it when the frost came, and then the dark. All those months and days of him having to stay locked up inside the cork were the cause named, vol... cane, as in, volcano. Which was what turned his fortune tide from the past. "Hail, no." "Yes, go." So now he must go back out and try to get it. Get it out of the very pocket, if need be. Out of the pockets of those other thieving "others" who want it, to feed me. But those who want it are also those who know that if they're to go out and get it? They've also got to give it. Well, let me try to say it a bit better, so you may understand more clearly, the letter. See those squares over there in that place where they are now, in the new estate on the bare-naked rows they'd plowed? They may be there looking up at the flying eagle's stare, yes. But this new place won't be bare nearly as long as theirs were yearly, in the dawning years. They want a lot of things to get done and to do, and lots of money to get such things to happen, too. But they are also the kind of people who know the queue. They know that, for them to be able to go on and make all of the "lots," like, the whole lot of money that they want to make to be funny, for a laugh, you know, no mistaking that, Honey. To be able to get all of it "got," you know, like, the money that they envy? If they're to get it. They're also going to have to go out and spend the little pennies that they already have, if any. But there were many of those with the "little pennies" in the pocket of the denim. Those little bits of such could turn out to be quite a lot of much for them in the Penn Inn. Kingsley would have clutched at his luck, then came the rushing, windy bus to go out and get the things that they wanted to crush, like... Like, the things that they wanted to crush the most, so that they could get their cut of the "Much-much toasts." But as it was to be seen, when such things started turning over, and out, on the revealing. Those maverick squares over there in the bare fields, those readying themselves to go out and plant fields on the new "bear" land, too, were very real. Though those lands will not be too bare anymore, like you. They wanted laborers for the fields, for sure. Bingo, now, watch the king go, and the rest of them, too. There they go, riding the flow of the winds upon seafaring tides. "Now, hop on, and let's go," said the king to them, "Let's go for a ride." They would have gone where the thieves usually go to play, you know, yes, now he's got it in his back pocket, flow. What with them having all those ships, and them now knowing the gear shifts of how to rock it and go, to get to it and to get it back to them quickly (quick), you know. This is certainly going to be it, "isn't it...?" "Yes." As for all that money, the other square men there already had the itch coming. Yeah, man, they were aching and itching to go out and spend it quickly on them. They were willing to spend a lot of that to have for themselves the "much more" that they wanted and lacked. Kingsley's got it: the things they lack from the locket in the backpack, hit. But if he doesn't have it yet. He knows how to go about on heat, as well as where to get it from meat, with a grab. To come on over and give it to me, eat, you bet. "Yes, my friend," said he to the rest of them; my friend, my good friend, is back in town again. To put you on your — "Hay! Enough of that man, now carry on without the rest of this song."

"Okay, Mom." It was to be the best of times for Bungie and his men, yes, those kinds, as well as those kings of the Kingsley times. It was the culmination of several things that brought about the current sin Ting, wasn't it something? Yes, something wasn't going to sit too well, nor was it going to settle well with some other well-positioned, well-thinking thinkers. No Siree, not after the arrival of those bearded drunken drinkers, and me. Because the Squares' king would have gazed out across the waves of the sea. That's when his eyes were opened up for him to see. Now look, he's looking out and seeing what lies out there across the deep from his boat. All those possibilities for those who will dare to come and see, or for whoever will go over there to keep the bee on oats, you know? Like, to go beekeeping, and to take hold of the fat chance at stopping from being anything such as these thieves. Like, to be there and working, and they did, Bee, no skylarking lurking there, like me. No, he was not sitting there on his apron strings chatting. Not like it was the custom with the other man, look at him, yes, that's him, a real whim. He was there, washed and wiped his handling arm strings after he was done with plating the sand and stoning the wind, as was his custom. "No." "Yes, got himself up off the bib, then went out and chopped down the very big trees. Then did more digging gigs yet, making canoes, boats, and shoots, like these." "Oh, shoots!" Yes, shooters were there, getting shot for not rolling logs on the shoots for handling very big ships in my youth. Big enough for men to live on the inside of it, all-inclusive."

"Cute! Cute."

"Yes, that's the truth, but living on in there for months and years on the average voyage there." Then across the deep, they sailed to where others keep their good lives living in peace, and they did. While other guys gave a bad life to a "Sifting sieve." They thought that was the must-have life to live, you know. "Ceet?"

"Yeah, man, I can see it."

"Nice, mi bred," he said, "go on, live it up..." yeah! Go "lively up yourself," and...

After they had risen and fought, and by fighting, would have won the right to control their destiny and might, Hingh. They wanted to control everyone else's, too. Even you and I, in writing, and a fist fight, as tight as glue. As for that man, the squared one, and his clan? He doesn't sleep and never learned how to dance on his own two feet; he's got two left feet when it comes to the dancing beat. But as for his head? Vibrant, vibrant is the name he has a brain. So, he's up there thinking again, even now, but not so when it comes to them, no, not the cows. But as it applies to Lars and his kind, friendly friends? "Mi blow-wow!" Look, he's out again too, but out to entertain you, and more "vain." Woo.

Bungie was a master at whatever he was after and had a cutting-edge buzz about what he did when he did. Until he didn't bother to do it anymore, and that was because he'd learned how to dot the "I's" and burn the crosses at crossing the "t's." At the same time, passing off the mental crosses onto us as laboring fees from thieves, to get others to do it for him. Meanwhile, look at him, yeah, man, you can still see him through the lens of this thing. He was there weaving netted links and channels that were all engineered from the top down to Crown Hill. Happened when he would have gone in and counted his brother's gowns, after they came to him, "Sit down." The answer to his "from higher up" calls, calling for them to come over and sit with him in the halls. Just to chat, you know, and throw some talk around in the rings with his many balls. So came they to him, all of them, like seven, eight, nine, and ten. He then went into the wee den, dragging them in. Into where, before those times, they had hardly ever been, like in front of him. They loved him, yes. But such brotherly love was four D best, if only for what he did, and he would have been still there doing such kinds of things for them and all the rest. Up until the final morning, near his headrest. Doing so for all of them, in making them out to be better than all the rest of the men. If for no other reason, they would have loved him as a friend; that thieving... No, that sort wasn't him, I meant to say, "That Bungie Stevens, thing." But for sure, they'd love him for some other real-life seasonal reasons, too. Some, such as for his efforts at making it rich and famous, for each of them, and yes, Amos, and the rest of the crew. It was his promise to them to pay the rent for his loving parents. His mother, the chief (chiefly her), was the intent since it was his scent that sent her away when she had to get up and go on the road, to stray. Toeing the way to go, under the load, but then... Bungie himself did not have much further to go on, either, other than to go the way of his beloved mother. While flirting with his purse-string at going the way of each mortal foe teaser, by toeing his way home. His brothers also had to do some goings and comings of their own; they turned around and went back home, to lay him low and down in his hometown, and then. In just about another ten, they would have been gone again. But as of now, look, they are there standing in his presence, squared, nook. Pretending not to like it there, and trying hard to deny it, the book.

"Oh, Lord!"

"Yes, Leonard, the Lord was eying the look that was locking itself upon the staring chord, in that little nook. It was not 'in the eye and be not shy,' like he'd taught them how to sell a lie. But they did; this time, they all lied; the stare was slightly off to one or the other side." Bungie was wise beyond his years; yes, he'd belied the years, my dear, but really, though. How did he ever get to become that quick on wit? He was the last of them, but first-class to all of them, especially when it came to the "knowledge thing." He sat them all down and took them to town, to go and school them on the real things that were worth knowing, as it pertained to the worlds of knowledge and knowing. Clowns were then crowning the times. "The time's good now to take a sip of the wine," he said. This time was showing up as his sign, even in bed. "This is the best time to go out and cast out the fishing line as seen through these Bungie eyes of mine," and he did. But then, when he was done, he sent them out, everyone, to conquer the world and then go beyond, to try and reach everyone who lived thereupon it, at the time. So, that's how it's been from then on: "Oh sheet." The world was his own and his beloved home. All of it, yes, he had no intent to quit, even though he had to go way before their time was over, his brothers were to continue, climbing up the ladder plan and hopping over the borders, but first. Let's see what's about to happen with the nerds.

They would have shuddered at the thought that he had gathered. Because they were there to find out what they needed to do there, you know, from the little brother... look, they're waiting to hear what they must go out and do. Like, how each of them would have to go out there where he was about to show, like... Out where he was to be seen, showing them now, to go, look. Peeping out now from the frozen window, look. Can you see it?

"Yes, carry on, carry on, if you can hear me and my dear lady, Mom, eat."

"Okay." Look, he's showing them the pointy finger; instructions will not linger.

"Now, each of you will have to go, um, click-click ...out there in the wide-open world, um, um, click-click, you know? To go and learn how to know, um, um, click-click, all of the deeper knowledge, and-and, and things profoundly fitting for the carriage, um, click, um, click-click. It's like this, boys?" he was saying these things across the long strings of his Bungie eyes. "Um, click-click, you must go out there and gather the things that are worth knowing, um, um, click, and then bring them back home to us to toy with." They were glad to know that they were being sent to go and for more reasons than one. But for none such as he would have had in the mind of the pan... um. He would soon be dead, though, and gone.

"To bed... oh, don't yawn."

"No, come on, man, not that one, 'At least...'" they said, sadly sad. Saying it one to the other "Nag" on the sob, "At least we won't have to bother to look upon the face of our beloved brother, beloveds. That alone is worth every dollar bill of his..." Still sobbing, even harder, but over chuckles and subterranean laughter. But they truly loved their baby brother, just couldn't stand to look upon his bladder there in that space, you know. Like, the space that was there upon his flabby face (so rare), yeah! Like, it was just hanging there upon his "big disgrace," well, so I hear. All the ugliness of the place where the parts were hanging above his waist. Below that, the leg was bent and bowed, and wobbly so. So, after he had to get up and go, and sadly so, they were all happy to leave and go.

"Even though they still loved him so — 'Oh no, not so.'"

"I know, I know." Would much rather if he were as rough and tumble as the others, you know? Like every other kitty cat kit, every other

the whole world over the saddles and bits. But he was not, and what was to become of him in things such as that? Speaking of others and the world over. Others knew a thing or two about the brothers. Like those (others over there) types of brothers. Other than the squares, and even the Circular ones. They were known as "The men on the moon." Chopping sticks and click-clacking spoons, yes. That must have been the place from whence they'd loomed, I'd guessed. Good for us and them by noon, probably, when the end shall come as a boom?

"Booming into the room, right?"

"Yeah, again we say, probably, because why bother me?"

Bungie's men were asked to go out. "Ouch!" Out and roaming about the rest of the route. The world at large would have known by then (no doubt) that the clan was out to wipe them out, and to learn all that they could gather from them, and at their expense. To take back the others' customs with them. To make them over into becoming their very own. Not as a brother, though, as it is known. So, they went just as they were sent, and brought back home what they had learned, to give it all to the gents and the rest of those kingly gnomes. To teach the same to the others of their very own and then trickle it down to the rest of their men. To help them become the greatest and strongest of the kingdoms yet. Trampling up and down, yes, but upon the other guy's neck. Right there on the other guys' doorsteps, even. They would have gone with a purpose in their palms, mining the minds of those other kinds. To learn and master all the other kinds, and collect the contemporary norms that were there for them to find, of knowledge in the arts, the sciences, and the crafts. As well as all of their cunning designs, since you'd asked. Bringing it all back with them, as a reflection of the customs, religious beliefs, and practices as they're taught. So that they could learn them, and then go out and teach such things in their home ends, of course. Taking it all away from the people whose seats are in the east and the west of their best, of the north. From wherever they might have gone in the best of years, don't far... Yes, that was how they'd come to know, and that which they now know has served them so, like, so very well. Even to this day, "What the hell!"

That meet-up there, though, was the last time all ten of them, including a dead one, were ever to meet up again together in one common place. All of them together in one open playpen of beloved brotherly brothers, "Now come on, make haste." But they were never really apart, just walking the path, engaging with the world in the smarts. While studying the arts, the girls, the crafts, the pearls, and the artisan. All that could be canned, they would have canned. They would have canned a candy man and put him in a tight-lid can, then constrained him therein, and stained him on the skin, yes, man. Then estranged him from his mainland unto a strange one, and another. Then yet another, never to get back together with his father, his mother, or his sisters and brothers ever again. "Don't mention it to them, though, not by name."

"No, man, I won't."

Now, let's carry on with the Bungie song, as it's known. "Oh, sheet! Look at this."

Bungie is now dead and gone, died there upon his bed of corn. The brothers would have heard of it and had to turn around and come back quickly that morning, his soul to seek. Had to see to the crip basket and the burial casket, you know. Their ten heads were hanging low, as the mock tears liberally flowed. If you were there and, let's say, you did not know. You would have been led to believe that they did give a cup of teeth to Bungie's closing off of the eyelids. Speaking of eyelids, theirs were heavy, under the guise that they were there pretending to worry. Worrying hard in the show-off chord about how it was that their brother Bungie was in such a hurry, hastening to leave from among them and go. But the truth is the truth, and it did show up on the young man's toe. Pointing upward and higher than it ever had before, almost as if touching up against the lid on the crip door. So, there he goes, showing off the rows, and then?

They would have lingered a bit longer. Like, like another ten fingers. Go on, count them like this thing goes: One, two... nine, and yes, ten.

But Bungie was not; he was dead and gone from among them, flat. They were staying over there together, but for the last time ever. However, they were to come running up headlong into one another's song again, though. But upon several worldly, bordered occasions to spend on go-go shows. They were never all together in the same time span again. Nor did they lose sight of the leger from whence came all the instructions to them from their beloved brother's braided head brain, as given to them. Carefully crafted instructions as to what they should go out there into the world and do, for him and them, not you. He was seen showing them exactly what they should do. They did what he told them to do and would have said before he was dead and gone to bed. That was what drove that generation's clove and was passed down to their children's hands in gloves. To their children after them, too, those present cubs, even. Yes, kings may come, and kings may go, but as for Bungie and his men. No, they never majored in the go-slow part of the show.

The Stevens household had become the sort of cornerstone of gold upon which kingdoms are built and told, and kings come to reign with shoulders cold. Yes, on such we are sold. The Kingsley King Squares, too, who later came to join up with them while partaking squarely in the scavenging scums of the crew, not you, though, no, it was just for them. As for the circular ones, whatever happened to them? Not much, nothing other than tough luck and biting the dust, as they must. Decreed by Kingsley, the king's kindly and timely trust. This would have been aided along by the Bungie one before he would have bitten the dust and gone. Way too soon for them and surely not for us. Now come on, don't yawn.

So, Bungie's men went out, per the words that came out of his mouth. They went out and about on the rest of the route. The world at large would have known by then, by the time they would have gotten around to them. They would have heard of them and their plans. No doubt, they would have heard that the clan was out to wipe them out. Because they were going about busily trying out their new fighting hands at things, such as winning at wars, so it would have seemed. Those

"Other people" would have known that they were no match for the coming sailors who were sailing in on them with the king's blessings, and the tailors' arms lengths, in the vehicles. To learn and gather and to take back to the others all that they would have learned from them, and yes, you, too. To teach others of their very own, and then trickle it down through the years, to the new crew. To help them become the greatest and strongest of the kingdoms yet, who knew! Yes, some of this was to be happening, right there on the other guys' doorsteps, beside you.

They would have gone out with a purpose in their palms, just as they were told up there that morning. Mining the minds of those other kinds, to learn all of the ways of those "Other kinds," and to try and master the contemporary norms that they were finding. All of the knowledge in the arts, science, and crafts, as well as their every design, as they were asked to do. They were instructed to bring it all back. Everything such as this, and that, like the religious beliefs, that were the prescribed feats and practices as it was taught, for them to teach. The winning ways and customs of people whose seats are in the east and the west of them. Wherever they were to go best, in the rest of the years, not anywhere near them, though. That's how they had come to know, and what they now know has served them so. Like, so very well, even unto this very day, can't you tell?

Something was going on, on each continent, far and beyond, at the time. Or not going on, depending on which side of the storm you would have hung the rod upon. Bungie looked out over the fog and saw the glad bag. That's how he'd tagged it and bagged the key to that which was limited only to what he couldn't see, at least not very clearly. So, he hopped up the path near the big tree, unsteadily upon his wobbly legs above the knee. Then ventured out a bit farther and very widely, well, comparatively, here, is the way we use the word "widely." Like, in the way it applies to his knees, one as opposed to the other, like these. When walking, you know, as he was beginning to get very tired and had to turn around and go back inside her... I mean, inside. That's when he would have lied and gone back inside the house via the side door. To "lie again," but down to sleep this time, my friend. But then, soon afterward, he woke up, then sat down to try and view the voids in the World Cup, of the scarred, you know?

"Oh, no!"

"Yes, the game was going on at the domes over there in town at the time, near his yard." But then, he turned up the teacup that was aforetimes, turned down on us, and then. "Oh lord!" He started out trying to foolproof the over-proof rumblings in the stadium and...

Hey, you, yes, you there, go. Go sit down over there and do some sit-ups to fill out the six-pack abdominal abandonment that you lack. Go on now, go, get it done quickly, and then come back here to me, okay? Anyway, enough of that sort of display. Let's go back to the Bungie one who would have sat himself down again, upon the coach wagon, to begin the split up and divide, as in the tasks that he'd hidden in the past. "Come on inside and sit down on your... I mean, as you're asked." Look. He hid it right here in his home, man, since you'd asked, yes, but now the time has come for him to share it all up among the two halves of his eight or nine siblings. Depending on who has the pen and is doing the writing, divide them into two parts among them, by him. He gave it all to them, to go off on a mission for him and them, "yes, along with the others of the have-nots. To go spy out the pied pastures green and all the in-betweens around those paths — "So, that's how his brothers were to have gathered and gotten themselves called up to the bed ladder, or something another?"

"Yes, like, like, to just come over and sit down and have a chat with him. So came the big, slow fall of the other 'All.' You know them, like, all of them. 'Them,' as in, those other men. Including but not limited to the Larries' den." Sent them out on ocean liners to go see what they could find and all things finer. He was so ugly, yes, brother Bungie. So ugly was he that, not even his loving mother, "lovely" Idi Hat, could have loved him cuddly, like that. Nobody could have loved him fondly. She did manage to live a little before she died. She'd lived long enough to have heard him cry, was always crying, as he grew on into his insides and outs. While he was going about grouting the oats, as into his wayward ways and his whereabouts, when and where he had gone out to graze by the wayside, dazed. Just a little bit bidden to abide by their days. But it so happened that, upon his doing the coming-in kind of thing, he would have scared the sheet off him and worried her rotten, yes, his mother, even. Even to death, not getting into the other (mad her men tall) medicine yet, that was the eventual bet, my brother. Yet he grew and grew to become powerfully and mightily set, as in, into all of the wealth that he would have gathered and gotten, yes. Such was found among the many things that he would have acquired and gotten. Growing strong often, and yet stronger, as he went "alonger." Yeah! I know, some folks are sure going to argue with you about this, as a show. For saying "Alonger," hiss.

"Instead of, along with her, perhaps, fist?"

"Probably true, miss." They're surely going to charge you, not me, though; I'm a no-show. But let's go on with the Bungie song, the solo. The world has a love-hate relationship with Ham, I mean, with him. Well, with that too, with both of them and you. Now you've got to stop this, children, and watch this sound coming on through.

The kings would have heard of him and were stiffly scared of the sin, you know. The very same wind that had befallen him upon his coming in was to have them blaming it on some sort of sin Ting, something. At least some of them were scared of becoming too friendly with him, but not nearly as scared as they were of being seen anywhere around him. Like, Kingsley, for instance. He was scared stiff of being seen out in the open square among friends while mingling with him. They were certainly scared of befriending him for such reasons. "The Bungie thing," as they'd taken to calling him in those times... no?

"No."

"Yes." Others, though, were wiser than those. They were wise enough to know to send for him, to get him to wipe his nose, and come to see them and make leagues with them. "To join up with us," so said the same Kingsley King, then in a curse. That would have been at the time when he sent messengers in saying, "The kingdom is much bigger than that little cubicle on the hillside over there, where you are staying, over which you now reign in fear and hide. Un-sober, growing your hair long, and steering your many and varied affairs in the wrong."

"Shur, um, click-click, um-um, click-click," he slurred the answer that he said to them and sent it back to Kingsley's men, the lancers and friends, really quickly, and then some. Forwarding it on through to the kingly monster, by them, trying to get them to go... or come. This means, in real people's language and terms, "surely, sure, I most certainly will, I shall be coming on still." Then he went in, and then came out again through the king's wide-open door, and had to be running away ever after from them. But not wildly as usual, and certainly not faster than the bore. Not like before, just running wide and wise, by staying on the other side of them, and their wise wiz-dumb. According to the way, at the time, he happened to see dumb, I mean, them. While staying away from them and where they are, at... at any time as given. Spending the necessary time peeping in at them and watching them feed and eating swine. Didn't trust them at all. Didn't trust anybody, nor their grind. He'd considered himself lucky to have gone into the king's parlor Dutty, you know? As in, into that dirty palace place over there in Sutton County. He was to think of it as a lucky draw for him, it would seem. For him to have gone in and to come back out again, and still to be found there wrapped up in the thin of his own Bungie skin. Been counting his lucky stars ever since, and even after thence. Yes, he's been counting; that was to become one of his favorite pastimes things and would become even more so. As we were soon to be passing off the many times he would just toss them out fast and even faster, in front of him in lines, and then start off a-counting mine; one, forty-two, more like a toy game for a boys' boy named "Bungie who..." Yes, he was just a tad lad like you, and yeah, one like me too. "Game," he is, and not to be that tamed, you see. But they're never going to have him standing up in front of them ever again to p... P, you know? Like, to be peeping back over the shoulder at them, just to see them, or to see if they're there peeping back at him in the wee den. As if they were trying to see whatever there may or may not be for them to see here. He's Bungie like that, slippery and cunning, and not too pretty sure if he knows a thing, or two, even four, or much, much more than you and I could put together to try and even the score. His other name was Stevens, right there before his reasons. In front of that is his Bungie, to plunge him squarely into the dungeons of the Bungie Stevens. "That poor, poor boy," that right there, my friends, was the real reason, on the ends. Oh, what a joy!

Bungie had some brothers, yeah, those brothers. That was before he'd turned around to look at himself and would have killed his dear mother. It would have started and happened in the process of him doing the incoming thing. Filing hard at filling out an over-taxed taxi taxing tax plan in the past and passing every other thinking tin man if you ask me. That's how he was to become number one. As for her, she was never the same again, as it occurred, until she was to face up to the end. The burden then fell harder and heavier to rest squarely upon his thin shoulder. Before he gets older, he must think about their future. That was what he did, and cuter. He went out walking (or trying to) while going about looking out and trying to find for himself the proper scouts to go off lying to. Doing whatever else it was that he did on the routes, in and out. Ever since then and after, while offering gigs and yet more gigging, didn't he? Yes, all in the effort at enabling squares and theirs, as in Kingsley. It was a miracle that they had met at all, due to the height of the retaining wall, over which he had to jump and crawl. Though the roads he walked were to cross the Stevens' set. They would have crossed paths with him, too, in secret. Yes, he and the King, and you. "No, that's not true." "Okay, go on through." Close enough to have missed each other by a split-second border crew, him and them. He'd managed to see them, as they came and went, in the evenings. But none of them knew anything about those things, and still — "How come?"

"What was that, 'How come?' you'd asked, my son; why was it Bungie and the king's men never did cross paths to face each other again?" A good question to ask of them, and since you've now given me the task, my friend? Let me try to remove the mask I'm in. It was because. Because he was a smart ask me no questions, my friend. My friend knew him then. But still. Kill that spill. It's because there wasn't a will; there was no need for them to go smoking weed still. The agreement was signed well and has a settled seal. Like, from a man in need to another's greed. No, wait a minute, Ingrid, neither of them was needy, buddy bud. No, not at all. Greed was the only scud, coming in to call. Bungie wasn't hungry, either; he was living fine up there on the meager. Lonely? Probably, but staying by himself humbly and homely. That's for sure, a good idea, homey.

In the beginning, there were two and three, then look, here comes you and me. One went out to try and outdo two and him, yeah, man! That would have been enough to make it at the other three that I... and she did the studies, studying how to show that she knew, how things worked, and how it was supposed to go. As for her? She did get things to work for him. Yes, not for herself, nor me, but for him. Those things did work and still will. Like, they will surely develop their working skills. The other one, though, her lesser brotherly flow, you know? As for him, yes, he went to work, too, but working for whom? Them, yes, not you. He was working hard, but only to pull up the ladder chord, "Oh, my lord," so he may become able to bother, "Oh, no, my brother!" Yes, to send his children to school, so they can study what that other man had made, out of fools, and rule. Then they, too, could go to work again, working for him. But then comes the end of one of them, and one is left to wonder. Which of the two will it be, my brother, my friend? I'm done.

8

Beam Weavers and Puppeteers

The old man was sitting across from them again, with his pencil and paper in hand, not the pen. Look at them through this thing. Can you see them? Yes: Beam weavers and puppeteers were there in the wee den, those were the good old days, you know. They were living fair and sitting in their swivel chairs; that was the order of the day over there. But as for him, he was not going to be there. Even though he was (in fact) a square, it was a rare situation where he used to sit atop the mountains up there. On top of the world, and not even seeing a girl that would, or could love him, good, just like she already knows that she should.

"Oh, no, that's not good."

"Yeah! I know, I know," but still, that was how it was going to be — Mister Wood, and Phill, for sure, until... He stared out the window with his Bungie eyes, now cleared, as he looked out and over the whole earth's spheres. That's when and where he started seeing things and what they might be worth to them, and to him. In seeing, he would have seen also some other fabulous things. Almost everything that was there to be seen, he would have seen, and even greater seeing there was to be, of the things to get from you and me. Because there was much more out there and over the other "there," yet he knew it. Quite unlike the other dimwits with whom we were dimmed down... Yeah! That side of the green pasture was rare. There was much to be seen by eyes that were keen and looking in there. He knew this, and that much. If he didn't see them yet, he knew he would come to see them later, you bet. Or he could go out to see them if and when he can, and he did, yeah man, that one was his can, can... He went out and about, manipulating things with his long eye-reach and very powerful arm strings. Soon afterward, everything was taken and gone away from them, like from the cowards and every other man around them, and was going to him to feed the rest of their mouths, around ten. Gone were they, further along to the other "them," also, like, to the squares and their kings. As such, things were just about to become the regular happenings. Although that was not his plan in the beginning. He did not include anybody but his Bungie in his first scheming. Yeah, that would have been him and him only; no one else was pictured on his pony. Nor were they mentioned in his planning session reasoning, Tony. But then came the intermission when, out of the hiding place, there in his stalls. Like, in the stalls up there on the square, where for a million years came the lusting calls. They started the call way up there, you know. Then came the tumbling downhill-fall flow that was to eventually have them squabbling among themselves over tiny things and the small.

"No! You mean..."

"Yes, but," loud and forceful came the whoring call. Came it not at them, bursting out from under the rug's sprawl, and as loud as the stink of a thousand what?

"Mothballs?"

"Yes, that — Paul." As for the others? Like the rest of the earth and the Hugh Man's all..., the whole of earth's habitation's worth was about to fall and feel the greed under his right, left-handed need. Upon his coming in, you know, the arrival thing. He would have been bearing heavy-duty, beaten steel. Metals of mass destruction in the deal, dealing it down upon them, everyone, he was never alone, though. It was he, along with the Bungie "One-flow." It wasn't just them who were in on the meager, like, on the plan. They were sure to have all the blessings of the squared ones, those who were sitting up there in the whole chain of command, even. After they were done beating up on the rest of them, you know them. Those thieving ones who were near them and were even found to be akin to their blooded squared-hue vein. They'd managed to get that far, ably aided along by the weight of Kingsley's weaponized bar, used as the tools of liberating fools such as you are... Hush, blow out the smoke, man; it's just a joke scam. But that would have been after the siren had sounded the alarm that outed smoking Bungie and all his ambitious qualms and carryings-on, as well as putting up with his greed and eccentric charm. Kingsley wanted in on all of the hauls, as was to be seen happening over by the falls. Asking little or no questions about anything at all, like how this, as well as all of it, would pertain to the conquering calls and exploits. Winning the world of all its might, and all other things such as the like, as if he knew from the beginning that they'd have to fight. So, the word would have gotten out of someone and hopped into the hearing aid of Kingsley, the king's commands. That was when he sent for him to come to them and meet up with them to plan. "To fine-tune and to make the mission strong," he said, "for everyone, and to our benefit." They were all to be part-takers partaking in all of it, you know. That was it; Bungie couldn't quit, or could he? Well, whatever there might have been or may yet come to be, we'll soon see. It was to be the beginning of the end for all of them and the other men, too. Like, those who weren't with them, mostly them, even those of the neighborly den, yeah man, you know them. They, as well as all the circular men and their times, must come to an end. Their endings had begun right there and then. So, they went out on the road again, and the high seas were to walk the board with them. With tons of heavy loads bearing down on them, my friend. They would have been wielding swords. Many were destroyed who came upon any of them on the journey of those globetrotting men of the lords. Those roaming, wandering, thieving squares, and then... Gone were all the precious corn and the most valuable ears. No longer feeding the hares, but gone, from here, and there, and from everywhere else. Gone over to all those squares over there, to go in and prop up all of their shelves, and soiling up the cups that were piling up on the gears on top of the Tupperware themselves.

In each of those destructions, the many culling events and other fan customs, he meant. Squares would have proposed to leave at least one. Just one of them was alive as it crossed their eyes. If only to go tell the tidings to other tribes around and about the drive-in. Yes, like, driving the fear of the gods of squares freely. The god of the squared king, really, driving it into them, all of them. Such was coming to be passing through the thoughts of his heartstrings, breaking and aching him, because he thought to himself. If they would just go away and die of fear, or vice versa, like dying of fear first, and then going away later. That would have been greater for those roaming crop takers. Half the squares' work would have been done more safely, sparing him a lot of "not." You know! Like, not having to do any of that killing sort for himself, or by himself. Not having to waste precious resources on those wasted waste people reclusives. But a mangy dog (they say) is better than a dead lion right away, and that is the better option for them on any given day. Every Lar, too, being a person of war, Sue. Small and insignificant though those wars of theirs might have been in the grand and ultimate scheme of worldly things to do, Lars knew such things. Lars and some of those very squares were to become friends here because they were to join together to beat back the Kingsley bunch, I hear. They'd met and gotten together over lunch, and that was where the intermarrying came into effect, too, upon the joyful bites on the crispy crunch, bitten and chewed. Then, over more sweating of brows around the drinking cups of warm, steamy brew. Like, the alcoholic brew that ended up affecting the objectives of the whole bunch, including you, no? "Yes, because I'm always this blessed." So, by the time Kingsley and his men got to them, to do them in, in the same way as they would have done to the squared one and his friends. Every one of those escaped Lars survivors would have purposed within themselves to stay "Aliver." Yeah! I hear you again, Mr. Driver, "This, too," you say, is wrong, my friend. But is it? Let's carry on with this sheet. All that was done per adventure, there should come another way someday thereafter, when and where Lars, just like squares, are. Will also have their time of fun in the sun, a time in the sunbaker, as they would have been thinking sometime later on. Sacking them down, like, way down under the ground. But will that day ever come? What will be the final outcome? Leave it up to none, I mean, to none of them, like, those gnome's combs, for instance. But leave it all up to the readers and writers, and the righters of wrongs beside her, and then some. Leave it up to such to decide thereupon, probably. But why bother me?

9

Climbing the Slippery Pole

These things came hopping in on them, on the very first caring night of those uncaring knights, again. They were climbing up the slippery pole, trying to get up the downhill slope that they were climbing, so we're told. But they did not know that was the hidden role that I was hiding in. Rolling the roles that each one would have to eat. To meet up with his God's teeth that I'm still wearing a smile with, while going to greet all of his preset goals. To be sold upon who was to be the god, chiming in, to redeem the soul from the Inn of sin. Each man… well, each person would have approached from diverse directions. Bearing heavy burdens upon his backside hung near the scarred section of the injections, as he was directed to do by the man when entering the chosen village and paying the king's ransom of a toll. "To get into the king's court and privilege," we were told. Which may, or may not be equal to everything he possesses, and to pay them for all that he was worth, and bless the rest of his nothings. So that it may multiply a thousand-fold and become something. But he must, if he wants to enter the carriage on the bus. If not enough, it is at the king's discretion a lot. Only at his discretion, perhaps, whether he gets in with an IOU offering, to get himself homely and into the town end. All this would have been made possible because Kingsley King squared had not forgotten how he had subdued the nation round about him, as rotten ass as… Chiefly circular folks and their kings. Just like his father, Kingsley ! would have done before him. It was now high time for him to go and gather the spoils and solidify his grasp upon the reins of powerful style. So, he gave them new laws, new rules, and a god to govern them, yes, those fools. Governing with the promise of peace, joy, and prosperity. If only they should serve and obey him, and him alone, not just you and me, Tony. To live by his rules; his laws and goodly god entities draw off; Jack as is, queens and kings, and all other beautiful things, only…

The only problem with all that, as we were seeing it, was that the gods could not speak for themselves, I mean it, mi cous. Well, so it would have seemed to that one wearing kelp, on the knee slip of his. While he's still sitting there and rolling his palm away at the weed stick and eating something, like salt mackerel with cornmeal dumplings. So the king had to speak for them, and to their help, in these schemes of royal things. In communicating the rules and the laws, he wrote them down to thaw. So, they came, coming in from all walks of life's vein… Vying to save and preserve what was left of their life "main." Trying to worship his gods, since it was made manifestly clear by then in those years that the Kingsley kings and their gods were a winning team. They were to drink to his fears like that, even in dreams.

Look, things are happening now; those trailers over there came trailing in behind the hidden cow. Many would have fallen dead in the waiting lines, and never even gotten close enough to see the behinds of… Never get themselves lined up there behind him, you know, like, to get in the mind of the king, or find a bit of favor with him. The dead bodies were to pile up and rot right there, wherever they would have fallen and dropped. The stench in the trench was to become just another of the many delicate intricacies one must pass through or has to endure. To gain access to the open door, to all of the king's many men and more, and one is not even close to getting to see the king himself, yet.

Inside the court, for those who would have managed to make it that far, of course. He must lay down his heavy burdens, like the sack bar of... of. It contained all the valuable things that he was hoarding. No, not as you are, but those. Those things that he would have gotten from the rotten..., something, and brought in with him for... His every earthly possession packed, or...

"What are you dragging that thing around and intimidating me for? Just do as you've seen the rest of the romance ticks doing, and you'll be okay, one shoe in."

"Okay, he, though, just the same as you, has got to lay them all down on the platforms on the outer peripheries of his chosen or assigned pole storm." Then, he must attempt to climb up the steepest of the greased poles ladder that I am on. After having gone through a myriad of initiations and orientations in preparation to do so properly. Hop on, let's move along, man, yes, mi papa, Leigh...) This pole that he must climb through is so designed as to bring him closer to who is to become his God. Since no one may serve two gods at once, he has to renounce and leave the gods of his past circumstances; those gods that he knew and had before times... in the past. He must go back, get them lost, and then come back, and that is because he must lose and leave those gods behind him for good. "Good." Very few were those who would have managed to make it halfway up the pole, let alone make it to the top, before they would have dropped and rolled. Dropping back down dead at the base of that pole, as said. So, the mountain of dead bodies would have grown and piled up high at the base of each greased pole, (wild). While the mountain of treasure that was to be accrued to the king's pleasure also piled up high, by every measure, or just by a country mile. Because every person must first bring their treasured purse strings in, then go lay them down before the great king, before he even attempts to climb up the initiation pole thing. At the top of each pole is (supposedly) where one might find his God, the goal. Then he will be able to go in and gain access to "life beyond life" for his soul. Few would have made it that far, and for those very few, none of them could ever return to their fellow travelers to be able to give them an insight as to what the best practices were to get one in, in proper order, to get all the way through, and to get home, over the border. The top of the poles was to be the crossover zones, you see. Points of no return for you and me. But it's also the gateway into the spheres of the great king, and the kingdom that's finally coming to him. "Come on over and be free."

Meanwhile, the king and his chosen men of valor were to wax mighty. "Like, if they weren't mighty already," and rich, too. But there's always a consolation for the great many, or even for the few. It's for those who never made it to the top of the pole but would have fallen dead in the effort, as we were told. Right there at the foot of the Polish to a shiny pole, squared. If one should perish in the pursuit, they were told. There is a day already set from somewhere, of old, for some time yet in the future, and in the great beyond, a place where and when those very same "some-ones," who would have dared to believe and rolled up their sleeves, pick up their belongings without qualms and go seek out the king's needs and come. Come take him up on his offerings of greed. They (those very ones) will be redeemed back to their god. Or gods, as the case may be, and in the reckoning. Well, to the newly acquired gods of the king, really, as in the case that I'm in, Neily. To his kingdom, to redeem their lives too, and to yet much more joy, pleasure, and satisfaction unimaginable. So said the king, his mighty men, and the miserable. But this is going to happen only if one believes in the king's definition of a Godly sleeve thing. Something that would seem to suggest to someone like me, and him, over there on the knee-slip. But not necessarily to us, we, and them. Suggesting something to the effect that the unbelievers have got nothing to worry about (in fact) to be free. But for the time being, they must do as the rest of the Romans have done. They must bring all their resources into the court of the great king, lay them down at the grey feet of the said great king and his carefully selected and carefully trained men. But then, there were those savage and barbarous nations and their peoples, who would have dared to defy the king and his one-sided decreed vehicles. They chose instead to keep and preserve their known ways of doing things, "Oh, please, you too?" "Yes, these." This stance was to have greatly angered the great king and his P... pea, peasantry, and that was the last thing anyone would want to be doing in those times. No one wants to invoke the anger of the kings in their lines. The king was very annoyed with me, so he sent out another decree: Forge this day an alliance with me, the great king of kings. Serve him and live, rebel against him and die, every last one of you. "Oh my!" Yes, so I heard someone cry, but... From the oldest to the youngest among them, and you, were about to die.

"But, but why?"

"*Mi nuh know*, man, I don't know." Not just them, though, but even the unborn in the womb, best of all, new, boom babies, even, not you. They, too, would have had a reason when they were to choose whether to stay or leave their mother's breast and go away. Knowing that that was for the best and for supporting their lifelong interests. Since everybody already knew that this king could and was known to have done it like that before, as he should.

"Or was it, like, like he should not? Like, like he should not have done it to others in the past?"

"I'm not quite sure about what happened in the past, so don't take me up on this task." Anyway, after knowing all of that, what do you think these nations and peoples are going to do first? Like, when caught boiling in such pickled stew pots? Well, at least some of them did; they'd picked up the teacup, packed up all that they had, and gone the Kingsley way to stay. Then there were the "lucky" ones who would have fallen off the great climbing pole strands and onto the pile of dead bodies beneath the folding stands. But they would have managed to make it out alive. Automatically, those were to become wards of the king to side (with me). They were then assigned a proxy guardian of the gods to manage them and their affairs, and then. They and their children served the king and his kingdom for scores of generations... All years. Yet there were others. Some of the others would have managed to escape the sword when the king and his bloodthirsty men went out to make good on the promises made to them by the lord. Like, to wipe them out with the sword, all of them, the rebels to scout, and to show them the end of the cords. A few of them did manage to hang on to the breath in their nostrils. But doing so only by their clever will, and by choosing to hide away in the coves of rocks. In caves, too, in hovels in the hills, and holes in the ground, right over there by you. Some even in the wet bellies of lakes and the ocean's wake. Which was to amaze the king's face and his men of faith, too. To the point where he would have spared some of them after they were found out and got their reluctant legs led in, to you. But for no other reason were they spared the begging season, other than to study them and to try and duplicate their methods and reasoning, but... Whenever and wherever Kingsley and his bloodthirsty men went in those days. Be it in the search for the rebels in the caves. In the search for new prospects in each case, or just plain out to wipe them out, yes, the devils. That's what would have happened to them every time; he would have wiped them out, and very cruelly so. Some Aboriginals and "first peoples" of some regions, as they're called for some reason. They were found to be mercilessly wiping their slate spick and span in front of that man and his ruthless, bloodthirsty clans. Many of them would have fallen onto the pierced end of the word, seasoned with gall. Others only happened to fall at a beckoning "sexy" call. While yet others were to rise to callings much higher, at the sight of a smoking gun and blazing flames of fire. Yet, Kingsley's desire would not be satisfied, or — "So, they lied?"

"Of course, of course, they lied, those guard-on liars."

"Oh no! That's not what they do. I'm tired (of you)."

"Oh yeah! I know, but I'm going to be here telling you about it, still. And for about a thousand times more, or two. Everyone knows that is true. Like, like..."

"Like what?"

"Like this, and that." Like, like how they tell you and me about the evolution queue when we all know in truth what they're trying to do. Now, tell me this, and the whole truth. If they, not us, certainly, not me, but they; them. If they did evolve to become something other than that. Or more like, to become someone other than how we're told it had begun. Like, to become someone more or less like a man, out of another brother, or even out of something else, like, out of another... Any other, for that matter. Like, let's say, just for argument's sake, let's say, it was out of a monkey. Or any other such kind of dumb donkey? Why then... why are there so many dunking monkeys still hanging around this donkey dump heap, and stealing away the people's food to eat? At what point in the timing scheme did they start rolling the joint and stop the evolving thing? Or did they? You tell me, Faye. But just a little bit of abutting butter here for the backside of your strut gutter, as you bounce along over this bumpy rut on your gut stutter. "What if..." What if that thing that you thought you were seeing, as it applies to the evolution thing, keying in? What if it should turn out to be a curse, and things like the truth are really in reverse, and the man was, in fact, the first? Like, a first-class and bigger boss. The "bigger bigger" bigger boss, and it was something that he had lost? Such things would have caused him to thaw and defrost, wouldn't they? And would have hence, have him start to disintegrate, degenerate, and devolve to become like... like a monkey? Solved. Why the hell does this idea seem to resonate so deeply on the inside of somebody and their behavior, mi pickney? Could it be? Could it possibly be so? Oh, no, my savior. So, tell me, that singing coconut monkey thing, like. That one over there clinging on to it, or the other one who's swinging off the limbs; the show-off that he is, hopping from one to the other limb of the coconut tree, you see. Was he right all along, looking like me? Am I wrong? Now. Sing the song. Yeah! That one, because this monkey right here? Has spoken his mind.

10

Gods Aplenty

L ook at them, they've got gods aplenty now, my friend, no? "Yes, I agree, so here for you are some more gods of worth, with great things to do, of course, for me." Like:

Gods of the new birth: Those who received the special gifts worship and do obeisance unto them. In return, the gods bless or curse the givers or those who dare to invoke their attention on behalf of others, like nonsense, just for instance.

Gods of the hurricane: They visit the people for good or evil, "to warn them or to bless, you know, no?" "Yes."

"Yes, it is the correct address." Strong winds may blow to send waste and withered things where they should go. However, when those very strong winds happen to be gods who will (without fail) show the enemy the road to toe, in. Don't get on the wrong end of their wrath, no, Hingh. Like, for example, when those very men were headed back home again, they were to run headlong into the fury of the Gods of the Hurricane, no?"

"Yes, and — "I know, I know." In studying things, though, he would have done the studies, and he was doing the experiments too. But that, too, was to study you; he's always studying you, and all of the other studded Lars studs too. As well as the unstudded buddies among them, and you. All this was done for him to try and understand all of the things they do, just as much as you do. Or fail to do as they would often do, failing to do what they were supposed to. In so doing, however, he was about to find out and learn more about you than the other. Much more than all the nothingness you thought that you knew, but never did know, in truth. That was just to show you that you did not know anything about the youth. You didn't know anything worth knowing, as the records were to show. But as for him! He would have known right away that you, Lars. You never did do "nuttn," sorry, I meant to say, anything, I want to... You never did anything in the cars, no. Well, not even in the cars either. I mean, anything of your own, and even though you may want them to go on and say that it's not so, Irene. You sure seemed to know how to go around and sew copies of other people's cows. Yes, that was how he'd managed to mop up your sweaty brows and harvest all the fields you had planted and plowed. Anyhow. There are other things too; yet some other fabulous things that he would have done to you, yeah, that's true. Things that are never going to be too flattering for you. Like, how he sells his craftiness and the bonding glue. Sold it, lot stack, and pork barrels onto you, and your nastiness too, came from, guess who? Yes. Things like... like those that you love to copy him and turn to do. He tells you how to do things, boo; things that you already know you should never do. But yet you do because it's new, sticking to him crazy like glue, and now, look, they're sticking to you, too — who knew? But as for him? As for that man? Listen on. The man knows what he's about; he comes over and stakes you out, to T-bone steak the lunch out of you, no doubt. He teaches you many things designed to draw you into the den, then into his behind-the-scenes sins, on the home end. He shows you around his shrine by shining the lights in and behind the walls of Kingsley's sparkling shrine... thing. All such things that are divinely designed for Jack as is, the mound keys, and swine. He designs them all to win you and your trust, too. Shows you what he wants you to do and tells the L out of the details, boo, saying that this isn't new, "It's the way to do-do booboo, and it's what I and everyone else do." He will even go all the way and show it to you if needs be, like when he's seen sewn onto you like seed beets, because that's not who he is. But you'd be like, like, you believe. Because you'll never really get to see who he really is, nor will you ever get to enter through the gates where he lives. Nor get close enough to the pastor to ask her what he's after. Hear that? Laughter, all at your expense, actor, after... After you're done pastoring off in the slaughtering, as if slaughtered off to the ever-after Inn. Yet more laughing laughter over there, can you hear? He's an actor playing the role of the movie clip scrolls, rolling the cow's cud to make the soup man glad in the paths out. Going to show off, the show-off he is, all those times, like when he was seen there rolling out the poster while casting broken bottles at the said cattle grazing in the pastures. Even if he should be consumed by the acts, Sir. That's not who he'd started out serving, and you will never have him become darker than they already are, Sir, quite unlike how such things are with Lars, Sir. He would have been collateral damage, a price to pay to get the real job done, and you? Down the drainage, for the greater image. The job of drowning and donning, you know who, and all of that man's kind friends, too. Your kind of "everyone," two, three, now, look at Mister Leigh, as in Kingsley. Go on, call him by his name, Kingsley; don't be ashamed of him; Mister Kingsley, king. Yes, him.

He has a purpose and reason. But not the same as those that he would have given to folks just like you, yes, and your kind, too. You just want to "up" and go off to heaven, to lay your head in the bosom of god as was given. Gods that he would have given unto you, and only for a season. To even you up after that time when you would have risen again, from a dead-end mankind. No problem. But as for you? Did you think you were on sparring terms with him? Like, that just like him, you're finally within? That you had managed to become equal to him, no, not yet, so. Like I, and m, maybe, img, oh my god, yes, maybe so, as in images to go. Images of him that he wants you to win. But not the real him: no, in this, then, squares won. Lars, your loss.

Now, here for you is a grab of God to serve, like Gods of the waters: Great to be on the right side of this God, if you want to prosper. You don't want to be found on the wrong side of her. Listen to what I'm saying while I'm here watching (you, praying), listening, and spraying a lot more nonsense in your hearing. Because while I was there with you and looking in at him, I heard you say some things as if you were there praying to him. In the form of a bow. Bowing down at the bowleg of his image that he has given. I'm now going to tell you something more about him. Look at him, focus the lens deep within. Look before you leap, and go take the plunge too deeply. Take things deeply into consideration, or you're going to mourn and weep, Leigh. Before you learn to swim, go for the grand slam to win, slam the man, thing. Now, I'm going to sleep. Because the still water runs deep. They are rising steadily and readying for the puddles around your little piedy (the feet). But when the rain comes tumbling down again, you're likely to get washed away in the flood drain and go spinning down the main. Today you're out again, though, still wallowing in the muddied stain and sledding in the snow.

Gods of war: Drives the fear of God into the enemy and delivers the friends to safety, yeah, where you are.

Gods of the moon and stars: "Twinkle, twinkle little star — "Twinkle little who? Why are you still listening to that, Booboo? Stop it, I say, just quit, okay?"

"Okay."

...

First, there were the Ovals. They lived over on their side of the oval. And the gods, too- his gods weren't a few. The Oval is a Lar, rounded, and Circular; that's how they as a people are. But not too grounded as the recorded sounds seemed to be sounding, and as they seem to be showing so far. All around him, though, they seem to abound in things spiritually unknown.

"Oh no!"

"Yes." But what is essentially central to all of them is a belly full of bulls and bears; the bare essentials, too, are there. The essential feat of majoring in all things to do with gods is to eat. But they knew nothing about these until they were to have gotten other things squarely foisted upon them, such as more of the same. Yes, you know them, more gods, my friend. Now they're found to have a lot of them there, and even in reserve. A grab of gods, yes, Gods to have and to spare. Gods to serve, to be served, and to serve up the mess, too, well, I guess that's true, like...

Gods of the ancient, Gods of the wind, Gods of the dead. Gods of the dance, Gods of the wilderness, Gods of the waters. Gods of war, Gods of peace, Gods of the new birth, Gods of our forefathers. Gods of the ancestors, Gods of the mountain, Gods of the valley, Gods of the moon and the stars. Gods of the fields, Gods of music, Gods of singing, Gods of shouting. Gods of the sounds, Gods of silence, Gods of trees, Gods of smoke. Gods of fire, and yet more gods are theirs to hire. And then, there are also the gods as given to them, which usually come to them straight out of the other guy's bag pen: gods that they will come and give to you and supply. Until you get yourself saved with all of your ssshheee shaving creams. Now, be nice and clean, and die, and go to heaven. To go and meet up with them, yeah, all of those that were given. Aah, some Gods, my friends, yes, as they are. Are they not?

Then there are ghosts, those who give the orders to the deceased to perform oats, and act as the spread upon your toast. Here come some more horses and their riders, holding on to the horsewhip on the gliders, and wishes of witches riding in on a broom. They may be found to be carrying something else in at noon. Like, when one of them was seen carrying the casket rim. Rituals were to follow in a particular order, toe-to-toe behind those with them on the border. So as not to offend or obstruct the journey further. The dirty duppy or the clean and subtle, yes, him, too. They all must stay at least a week and linger, following the commands of the Magicians' rings on the fingers, and you. While they were passing by the show-mourners there, weeping and leaning in on the window, well, maybe. "It's true." To carry messages in, on the return home journey, back to the fair lands of the great ancestors' home, to get home, Leigh. Carrying along with them the messages that were sent during the nine-day event. First sent from a period of mourning to the nine nights and up to the burial. It's an omen to those who love them enough to carry all. As for those who don't love them! The ghost will haunt them. But...

...

"Whatever happened to Clem?" "Mi gut!" Somebody was heard lamenting about these things in the hut. "He was the real king thing, wasn't he?"

"Yes, he was noble and very well-known, too, was he, like that."

"I know, I know." So, I'm sure you already know that he was not going to just sit on his backside down at the courtside and watch the wrist-watch, just to see what time it was going to strike the clock, bang, bang, and then sit down again. No, he wasn't like that." Some strange things were happening then, things that were going to inform him of many of the current slackening-up on important events, such as the state of affairs as it pertained to the present sphere. Like, where his young son, Elazar, was about to be placed in his seat near the super chair of the Lars, over there. He wanted to know right off the top of his brow. "What's to be coming home to roost on our tree stump, after that, I'd like to know, now?" That sort of thing would have been happening over there often, starting at the very time when he was beginning to see what was left of them. The other Larry friends, yes, those. He was concerned and wanted to know more about how they would have managed to be seen as faring so well among these strange men. They were beginning to be seen and counted in, numbered among those who had gone and joined themselves in the pack. To go off on a floating match down the river track. Like, when they went out and joined up with those squares from over there. They were seen regularly out there, wielding the spear on the quest of slaughtering off the lions and the deer, the birds, the bears, and the young millitier. "Where oh where did you get off your un-circular not-noble chair, to have walked a path that would have ended up here, lost, and trying to fit fast a rounded Larried pole on the inside of a squared assuming that the square pole could fold?" So he growled. But then.

"This has got to stop," he spat, and there too was where the chatting was to be stopping. The chopping ax was back and being sharpened. Whoever was found to be there, and was not Lars, but Squares, but were found sitting up there on top of the front cars, theirs. Just like that car right there. The car that he, that same "someone" personality, would have taken from thieves. If he had not paid the proper ransom on his arrival over here, for it in taxes and fees from the treasure house of his own forefathers' golden bar, like the thieves that they are, and which he would have brought in with him from somewhere over there on the other tar, to spend on one night of sin. Yes, a bar that he would have dragged in with him upon his coming in, if he had not parred the dice and paid a fair market price to win. According to the worth, what the real value of it was, and nothing less. Like, he'd better make sure that no less than the proper market price was paid up for it by him on that bargaining trade day, at the bargain Garden Inn. If "Nord…" which would be just a bit north of not. Then, the land did not belong to him, flat. So now, after this and that were checked out, confirmed, and settled upon as a fact (or not), look, the real owners will soon be coming back, purposeful and packed. Riding high with him upon the repossession, airy wind. Nothing wrong with that sin ting, something thing. He would have gone and done it and would not have quit and sat on it. No matter how hard they would have tried to spit, he would not sit. He would have gone and done it up until the split was to come with it.

At the beginning of that reparation thing, the whole den of Lars roundabout was with him. Even in the songs that they were known to sing. Which did the magic, and served him well to rise above it. Growing strong and blowing up steam in the trade winds, to raise him on the eagles' wings. But then, soon afterward, like, after those times, and after those things had begun to begin to come shining on the cowards, then came the days of slowing, as in, down again, and… Look, look at them. Those Lars, strong and mighty as they are, all around, "Men of renown," soon afterward, they began to go missing in action yards and could not be found.

"How is it going, my brother?" he asked the eyes of the hand-shaking other guy. But brother's eyes would have bowed over to kiss his slumping shoulder. Brother King was older, so he knew right away what the odor of the soldier was. He knew right away that his brother now sells boulders to his other beloved adopted brother, who lives over yonder, beyond their border. Things were going out of order, as seen through the eyes of a real man and a father. He had (obviously) gone and crossed over the soft shoulder and was now wrestling with the squares over there and with that man's Cobra. But as it has always been with that nation's father, it's not over until it's over. Not as it pertains to this old soldier, and his needs at kneading the dough, not at this point. So, he reached for her clover and held her much closer. She was his beloved Larry neighbor, his beloved homeland, in his favor. He began to fight the plight of his ailing might, up until there was no more fighting will left to him, there in the money till. But still, he was to have them killed. But not all of them, because, as you already know, they're very cunning people in the running vehicle. They're always on the run when the hot oil "catches a fire" in the belly of the boiling pot. Like, when the heat gets turned up really hot, that squared thing will not be anywhere near the pot to partake of the stew like that, along with me, and him, or even with you, watching. He will be long gone from view, sending others in to do battle with them and you. But while the victory is new and the victor, not yet renewed, in strength. He caught a stink of that other man's scent to that man's own descent. That was how Clem went, never got back on his feet again after his beef with them; he was spent. Now, Sonny Boy King, don't ever forget the innate wayward bent of that squared one. Remember, he never repents. He could easily have won and should have, man. If only Larried sober were to side with their beloved brother who lives by them on the border, but "Tuff luck." It was not going to be the stop for that buck. It wasn't all their fault, though, that they were found at fault on the slope. They were pushed on the tumbling; in so doing, this would have been the push button that had gotten him overthrown. You know them, those square men? They were all up in there, even those who were on the outside of the square and looking in. As usual, yes, they were in there, doing whatever they must do to make it clear to anyone who may try to do it. They thought it was all mutual. If ever anyone should even so much as think a stink thought of such things again to do the sort, they would have been doing such only to be reminded of who is the boss. They would have been quick to find out what happened to the kings who dared to try and fair it up with him, as they have done in the past. That's how they'd come to know these things. That right there was to become a constant reminder to them of the wonder-working wares of all those Kingsley Kings Squares. But the Lars brothers were about to throw him under the bus, to get run over by the "other," no, not us. But as an offering that was offered up to them for slaughtering in the house of the wolves, for thousands of bellies full. Yes, full of three "squared" meals a day. By playing the easy squeeze tease, they went away, siding with the dirty money pay, okay? Anyway, then comes this new day, and one might have heard what those children have to say. "Now is the time for us to stand up in line and go take back what's really mine." Have they not seen the sign? Brother, be mindful of how your forefathers had signed the dead-end deals. Never forget how they'd sealed their destiny into perpetual poverty, even to the deathbed, among the seals. Don't go about walking blindly, thinking that they will treat you kindly and fairly. By saying that "this is a new day, in the new year," no, not so. They won't go slow and allow you to hitch a toe and get to hop up onto the bike that the man had already spiked to prick you in the dike. Not only does it apply to you. But to anyone else who would dare to embrace the psyches, to do anything such as these...

After a retreat of the Lars in the streets, Squares were about to run headlong into more defeats; they were having difficulties with the wrong scars, again. By going around warring with other Lars and friends. Lars, who was there cleaning the toilet bar and minding the square's babies but... but. But today's music, they say, has more dance than University.

"...oh, what the... You mean, the university has a dunce?"

"Dance, I said dance-oh, not 'dunce.' It's not too far-fetched, though. Come to think of it, this could be where they sit," since every-where one looks, one is likely to see such kinds of things, like... Seeing them there carrying books, like me, and taking on the strangest of looks, but still can't see. Digesting what their mama never cooks, while their dads walk across the cranny and straddle the nooks, wondering who it was that had baited the hooks to reel him into the waste disposal bin. But then again. Continuing in Larry King's commands is where the issue rightfully belongs.

It was the time of the kings; yes, they were all there, just chilling on either side of the den. Over there were the squares and their kings; they were very fair. Well, so they liked to think. On that other side, over there, too, was the Lars. Just like squares are, Lars and their kings were also fair. Like Larry, for example, the newly crowned king of the circulars, those who had long lived in peace beyond the wooden bars with their killers. Yeah, man! That would be them; they were fearsome warriors and mighty men. But then came the times when, upon the growth and prosperity of the civilized man, yes, he was among the very first of them. He had to look out and about, then yet out much further around the boat. Trying to find the correct answer to the looming doubt. To maintain and sustain his growing civilization as in the days of the former. Trying to shore up his power base, you know, to try and disarm her. He started to flirt with the high seas, where he ran headlong into these squared peoples of the northwestern higher seas, and then. After they ran into each other there. They started studying one another's spheres. Well, one was studying the other, but not the other, since only one of them was ever known to be studying anything, like the brother. They were brave and fearsome warriors, though, as many kings were to come to know after they were made to pack up and go, like, back to where they first bent the bow. In practice, as I thought it was, in the snow. But what Lars did not know was that the war was never over. As is the norm with the squares and the sober, their other brother from another mother of a... anyways, there's always a war going on where, like. If they're not out fighting the battles, they're sitting down and making the plan; their victories are not measured with the man or even with any particular nation. It is worth the entire Kingsland world, the KD's kind of human habitation in his hands, girls. So, he fights on, winning incremental victories that are far beyond the scope of the other's visionary derision.

"I see," so said he. In a thousand years from now, though, he will be like, gone. But he carries on as if in command. His children, though, somewhere down the line, will meet up with the man's mind behind a bent bow. In their own time, even, to go contending for the sins of their forefathers' blind season. Or for not reading the sign, Eden. Now, these are the current happenings of popping the champagne and drinking expensive wine; this right here is that time. Looking back now, and seeing things. Like, seeing squared fingers pointing back at him. No, not at you; you're okay, Boo. But at him. He's sitting there in the rocking chair and laughing. Yeah, man! That's what he does, often. Yes, he laughs at the glorious cost of his own sin that the other king had taught him and won — "Don't you mean: fought?"

"No, not fought, but taught." He was done with the fighting, as it was with the talk show thing? He was done with that a mighty long time ago. Starting when he'd learned how to win, by his studies up there in the snow. By doing the teaching too, and the un-teaching of you, and then re-teaching other men's sin Ting, some things to his crew. Leaving his fight up to others like him, and them, up to you and your brothers, even. Didn't he send you over there to fight wars with "Spear him, mi Lord, oh, spear him?" To win the victory for him and the glory, too?

"Yes, but, but."

"But nothing; you did the fighting and won, but all the glory went to him, greasing up his palms. Glories that they seemed to think never belonged to you. But guess who? Well, who knew?" Now that you're like, you are done with fighting them and with winning and bringing all the glory to him, in his might. It's now time for him to do you in, without you even knowing a thing. But he's there doing it all in rights, yeah, right you are. Yeah, man! Like, like you not knowing what it was that hit a whack upon you, right there, amongst the bugs, yes, man, right there in the right eye... "Sight?"

"Seen."

Well, alright then. You're mighty neat with the yardman, Sin Ting. There he is, my friend. He's back to teaching things again. Teaching you how to go about doing yourself in, without anyone else even knowing. So that no one can point a wagging finger at him in that blaming thing. He's out there peddling death and destruction as a jet set. By being passionate about fashion, 8, and all that is there to get. Passing it all off to you and me, under the guise of law and rights, booboo, bumblebee. Right to do wrong, not what's right; selling you nasty and deadly sins to eat and bite. Dealing you with death under funny lines and grinning teeth half-white, and you go right along, singing the sweet swan song. There's nothing wrong with that *yah yaad man*. Because *weh done dead-arreddy*, yes, I knew that already, that is what I thought you might mean. He owns everything around you. Controls the media, too, and tells you what he wants you to do, and you do, do. Do. Until you are screwed and unscrewed. Look, he's there screwing the L off the bottled brew even now, like he's always been known to do. Did you ever stop by the Jin to do that thing? You know what I mean, like, the thinking sin ting, or any other such thing? Like, to at least try to know and get to understand how things really are, and get done with that man, to be gone far? You do know how things seem to change with him, right?

"No, I don't."

"You mean, you didn't know? I know. That's why others are bound to have to tell you so, even others like me, you see." Like this. "A time and a season," they say, "for everything to play." The time for the "building up" of you is now all done and gone away, so now. It's time for the other end, the breaking down again. As it is with him, the other men's mighty man? Now, this wonderful, marvelous thing at which you're looking. It's the time of "breaking down" of you keying in for him, under the guise of "rights and freedom ring." One day, it is a deadly sin to even say some words to him. But on the next sunny day, it could become quite okay for you to speak and to say it that way. Saying those very words to him as if to pray. Not to mention the other new inventions, those that are not that much of a news to mention, like how you now have all the rights to go out and do what, tonight? As for you and me, too, in the meantime, what do we do? Well, let me try and see if I can tell you in the same way as she did to him, and yes, guess who?

"Go over there," she said, "I want to show you something out there, mi bred."

"Go, go. Go over where?"

"There, over there, now look at it, can you see? Look, look at it, man, not me, nor the hitman" (can't see). We dump our resources over there. Like, whenever we dump it and other such things, like junky spunks we want to wear. Instead of on our children's brains under the expensive, extended hair. With our neighbors, too? Just the same as you. We drink more expensive wine than Mr. Norm Francis. Drive more expensive cars than Mister Ital Leon was, or is, and go about wearing more gold and bling than that b x thing had ever had in. Oh, my lord. Oh, my lord, what shall I say to you? Other than to tell you. Stop investing in his dump yard down your lane. There are those you know who are arguing over the name, saying the two are one and the same. You know, both of them, as in the dump yard and your brain. Go, go now in your once awesome name, go make a liar out of that mighty vain. Show them where to go "fall" the rain, if you Cain, or Able. Can you make the connection? Does it connect yet, my little pet? Have you seen yet which of those cats to place a bet on? Go to their schools and universities, too. Learn the rules; they'll teach you fools. They'll give you tools and "how-to," but will never give you the purpose to know how to know for us. Nor will they show you where to go for the bus, not at all. But a bus is as good a thing as a drive-in to go for the books, no? Yes. Except where it's good for them and their friends, and when you're there playing with their balls. Majoring in the minor leagues, that's all. But one thing we've got to learn is a must. We need to learn that that will never be good for us. So, the very first thing to do after you are done with pulling the purse strings on his fuss. You will need to shift the focus towards knowing how to go about building up and securing the motorbus that will carry us to our ultimate goals, plus... In other words, built by us, for us, and then, when we're done, we may go out and sell the leftovers and the surplus for a hefty sum to them.

Yeah, man, wordplay is the order of the day here, too.

11

In the Name of Larry King

It all came about and began to happen to them first, in the name of a Larrie kind of king, of course. It was the time of the kings; yes, there were very many of them. Over there were the squares, and their kings were fair. Look, on the other side, over there are the Lars and theirs, even now. Just like squares, Lars and their kings were also fair. Lars, though, as things were to go, was being studied, but not knowing a thing about these, like his buddies. Like is the custom with things when it comes to him. Those rounded, circular gentlemen never bothered to study anything. So how could Lars have known that far, to have known that some of them were merely clowns, not stars? Acting the part, unknown Mister Mistar, for the greater good of...

"What? The greater good of a squared house and home in the hood?"

"Well, yes, of course, that's good." But there was one Lar who knew them from afar, and he was different because of a scar. He knew enough to have known that he didn't know a thing, nor even two, or thirty-three. So, he would have proposed it on his knees to go out, learn, and copy the already established normalcy. Trying to learn as much as he could, turn around and gather, or scatter and burn it all on the altar, made of wood. Burning all the wrongs that he could get his hands on, from the other brother from a mother of... or even to that which he could not earn, he was to turn, and that was when it happened. Clem would have caught the vision, but the rest of them never did know his decision. So, they copped out and let him go, even to prison. They'd tossed him into the lion's den, you know, of the wolves. Then went out to play golf, basking in the things of the other guys' sulks. Sulking in his bulky kind of hardware, soft, and drinking expensive wine, then turned and took a wide-eyed look into the glass and dined. That's where they were to find those finely cut suits of the bespoke kind. Then got spoken to as an eloquent stooge. Smoking expensive cigars and often offering booze. Boosting the imagery down the slippery slope of foods.

"How in the world could something like this have happened?" He scratched his cap-stand and wondered out loud at them. Although he already knew that he was not allowed to talk out loud in a crowd, he did so anyway, children.

"Okay," I heard her say, "let me try and remind you how to remember." She said this, fully awakened now from her slumber; instead it's... She then went on to deal him, with a spread when she had to open up to him in bed, and further said: The squares would have wandered in, driven hard by the fearsome rushing wind. You were the king then and reigning over them. You were mightier than all of them, if you ask me! But wait a minute, you did ask me, didn't you? Yes, yes, you did. So, I'm going to continue telling you whether or not you want to listen and obey the queue. Like I'd always say to you, don't ever go down to Bay View. Even so, I'm telling you now a bit more of the score, like I was saying before. You did tumble down upon him and waged war with him, and won. Yes, you did win that one, yes, man. But that never-give-in, never-gives-up thing? Never stops losing until he wins. Now, this wonderful, wonder-working thing at which you're looking? This right here is him, winning again. Have you been listening? Have you been paying the proper attention, oh, my Larry King, and my beloved companion? Because if you were, you would have noticed the vision. That which he would have envisioned from way back over there, where it all began. You would have also come to notice that the squares and those kings of theirs were going everywhere in those days. Everywhere they went, they were doing "bad," oh, my lord. They never quit, my lad, no matter what it is that might hit them; they're always coming back again mad, as mad as, well. Placed one of their own in and among the local folks, and then another, and then another, and then, by the time any of ours could heave-shake the shoulder and say, "Why bother... with them?" Squares were to be seen there, taking over everything and running all over them. Pushing the locals out of the evening (out of order). Overwhelming them and getting them to quit and change all they had ever known and done. Then went about quickly replacing those with new and strange other things and other "some-ones" like their sons. Having them call it "good, and a blessing, and betterment." This would have meant that by the time they were to know what it was that had bitten them, they would have been cast out of their tents, and squared faces would have been in. This is where we are now, Sir Larry King. But really, though, come here, come a lot. Come on, man. Let's sit down and chat. No, leave out the chit, no place left here for that shit. What kind of people do things like this? Like, sit down and take a back seat in the train on the track rolling down the round hill station-bound till, like, until he is done with paying the bill? After he's dead and gone, his descendants are left there praying on and paying them still? Who was it that had broken your will? How is it that you should end up like this, Bill? Like, where other men now tell you who to kiss, and you go right on out doing it as if you are being dragged to the piss pit? But wait a minute. What's this? Oh, that's it! The pit- that's it right there, no? Look, look. You're lying with your back down over it, and not even realizing, sit... Sit up, man. Sit up and talk to me. Where's the beauty that we once knew? Where is the vibrancy in the spit you spew? But that's what usually happens when one would have forgotten, you know? Like, when we forget not to let other people's rotten... become our prize. Like, the price they pay us for picking their cotton and sifting out the rice. That right there was his key to come over and dump his strangeness down on you, and on me, too, nice, yes, but wink-wink and shut up. That, I suppose, was because my father's, I mean, our father's ways were not free. Now, can you not see it? Can't you see what has come upon the entire family, knee slip? You do everything now for everyone else's comfort but ours, and according to their programs, go, try, and score yours. Including sparing the rod for our children's bad behavior, man! What's wrong with that one? Yes, that's it. Because he tells you that that is Saddam bad, I mean, too damn bad. Although it's him, yes, that very same man, thing. It is he who is going about splitting them up and tossing them away from the life of living with their dads and moms' song, singing. As if that is a good thing, and not wrong, oh man! Now, can you see? Sit, sit up, and look at me. Go spew some spit if there's any venom left in your slit; do that for me. Could it be that was what they were out to get out of you, like, like, from when the day was new? That would have been on the day when they'd happened to bump into you, and yeah, me too. He was quick in putting on the journeyman's shoe because the road was so very long that much he knew. But as for you, and yes, I know, that includes me in the queue. We never knew what to do, it would seem, even if and when we should find out what to do, even if in a dream. We were never found to be able to follow through. Woah. How screwed are we? Who is he, that person or godly entity that is going to be able to save a sable like me? Like, who's going to save us now? Wow! They're out to get us, can't you see? Like, they want to get us out of the way. Yay, stay there with all of that glare on your staring pair. You know, like, on the "eyes" things. Even more so than him is the "vision" one. Come on, wake up, man, wake up and come along; we've got a long way to go if we are going to continue to go on. Or to get anywhere, hop on; we're going over there. Speaking of hopping on. That one? The square would have hopped a ride on the wagon over here, while on the route, going everywhere. After having seen all these fabulous things in his dream, and a lustful look at the can of beer. He wanted them, "all of those things," said that same square-faced Ben, I want all of them, and they would have laughed. But Kingsley King wasn't laughing, no, not at all, my boss. He was as serious as a fall. It was as if he was falling from Grace land "dead" bouncing ball.

He'd opened up his eyes and looked around the saw. That's when he would have seen what he saw. Like, Lars here walking on diamond-studded ground straw. Rubies and Jasper, precious gems, prosper and abound in the raw. He wanted it all, even the ground itself, to build up his stall. There were yet more precious things lying around out there, too. All there in the ground were valuable treasures unknown to you. Back home over there in the "Frigid Zone," though, they knew. Soon afterward, they were there prophesying the profit they would be buying with your bloody bleeding siding.

"But he lied then. Didn't he?"

"Well, of course, he lied. But as for you, what did you do? Sit still on your backside? Yes, you went right along singing the hop, happy apathy song. All night long, my child."

At the beginning of the charter, Clem was smarter. He would have known that he must always remember. He doesn't fight well with fat; he likes to stand up firmly on the flat. Well, to tell you the truth, he doesn't like it when he has to fight on the water boat, either. But he was eager because he also knew another thing or two about the in-breeder r..., I mean, the top class (clown) of a man, of the century. Like, what they were after, and since they had come that far. He was sure that they were not going to turn around and part with the walk-pass. Well, not without even getting to have a little chat and a haughty laugh with them off-hearts, like, with us, with you even. On the Larrie bus, with my friends, in the evenings, and so on, on end. He would have known how to make them go easily. Or let them come in hard into Larry's boneyard. "Come right on in," he beckoned to him. He would have chosen the "in," you know! Now, come on in a bit closer to me, he said, to Kingsley, the bred... "Come on in, Mister King, Mister Kingsley King." Well, it was not really to the king that he said it, but to his men. They were his loyal men on the maritime, but then, later on, Kingsley was to take the invite and come over, too. Then, that was when it happened, no, not to you, but... They roped him in, dragged him, and then bagged him. They'd wanted to flog him, but some tender-hearted someone (as usual) would have begged for him. So, they washed him instead, then fed him, and then went out and about to try and bed him down for the evening. But not before he was entertained and got himself stained with the remains of his drain. As in, the way he was draining the drainage piping down the main, and out again came more draining, from around the backward bend, even. It was as if it were raining over the king. He was dripping hard and wetting the wipes he was given, which were soon tattered with various colors before their eyes, even. Look at the pores, "Oh, the poor thing." The rain was falling, just like water; it was pouring from his pores, and from farther away. The watery substance was pouring, yes, showing up on the right side of him, and all the mess. Then came the sobering up of the brain; right away, they would have been back at it again. You know, back in the game, playing it again. Well, it was their game, not ours. Not our game, no, but theirs, of course, "the squares sugar cane game," was the name, as they'd called it. Yes, that said game. As for them, as for those Larrie men? They have not seen a soldier called "sober" again since. Or have they? Before he could have chased them away, though. Those squares were beginning to notice the latter end of those Larrie men. He now calls them his friends, yeah, that would be both of them, Clem and Elazar. "If I can't beat them now, I'll join them," he said to those with him in the car before speeding away up ahead. That was when...

He went about making leagues with them. Invitations were to be sent, got sent out to get visits from the visitors, and the reverse of this, the hearse, was to be the next verse. He never bargained for what was about to befall him at all, as he was to recall it coming in from the higher-up callers' calling for the fall. Well, not him; he would have been gone by then. Like, at the end of the ending, he went to the hurt of his fallen, calling back with a warning by way of the spirits. His dearly departed spirit was calling them to attention from behind the other dimension. But no one seemed to be listening to them anymore in those times, let alone paying the necessary attention to the warning signs. They became close friends, though. Too close for comfort, with which Clem was comforted on the way to go. Up until the truth of Kingsley's boot was to walk the route, and all that once belonged to Clem was to become Kingsley's loot, or worse.

Clem's advice to his young son while walking the slow path home was the same as he wanted to pass along to the next in command. While still lying there on the dead-end bed with his head down near the crook of his arm. His advice to him was. "Don't take craps from people. Not even for once, no, because the minute they find out that you are the person who will take it in on the vehicle going down to the market-place. That will be all that will be coming at you in the thereafter kit case." Now, will he? Will the young king remember him enough to heed the warning from me? Good night, and good morning, depending on where you are now and reading this storm, Hingh.

Kingsley went and sat down in his cabin far out of town. All wrapped up in his favorite house gown. Then he began on the doggy hound, "To a world unknown," he said, "here I come." If I want to claim the land, he was heard saying further on. I must first be sure to have a plan. Then another, and yet another one. Then just stick and hide them somewhere in the pillar casing near the house-pan, just in case you know. Can't just go in and slaughter them all to waste and go, take everything that belongs to them and their taste, no, then turn around and leave again? Well, yes, I could, you know! He turned and said to the bro. I've done it many times before. But not on such a massive door, and surely, not on a single score, no. "I know just what I shall do. Those Lars won't know what hits them and, yes, you, too." So, he did what he did, and all of him and his doings are happening still, even now. Wow.

Once upon another very long time, like, when he was looking up and out over the hairless heads of his godly spread, not mine. There he was, Larry King, not the tugs, looking. Larry King began to find that he, as well as all of his kind, had fallen far behind again. Way too far for him, as a matter of fact, and them. He, too, just like all the other Lars, had again fallen way behind the cars. "No, I know, it wasn't those; there was no such thing as a car anywhere around those parts then, on the roads."

"I know, I know that too, but..."

It happened around those same times when the carts and those riders had gone carting to find her the sider. He knew right there and then that he was going to have to get up and get moving, to continue being the chief provider, with a shoo-in. He had to go out and spend the necessary time and overtime. That was because he knew he had to catch up in line with the rest of mankind. He ended up making leagues with this young Kingsley. But only after they would have taken to crowning him king, Kingsley king. His wrong call was about to come calling, but never mind, Hingh, he's all in, has surely got the time. Kingsley King is in no hurry to begin to make him worry. That's not how the Kingsley Kings roll. Unlike how things are with you, him, and them, a member of the household. Kingsley has got a lot of timing in his soul to spare and spend.

...

The beginning of the ending. The young King was carefree and careless, too, like me. Until he was scared stiff, just like you. That's when fear left, and popped came the spiff out from the front side of the splits. That one right there hanging out at the halfway zip of his tunics. Which, at the time, was seen spewing awash with rats like volcanic ash onto the blue vest. Oh, what a mess! All this was to be seen and commented on with such responses by some of those who were there with him. That was a day of great trouble for them. Kingsley's knees were too wobbly, my friend. Or so it would have seemed to the other men, who were there with him, and tugging along with the one who was writing the texts with his pens. That's what was happening there the first time when he was hard-pressed to go take a peek in. He had picked up the book for a look at an ancient family recipe for cooking that evening, you know. For another chance at a look-up of the reading before he was ready to go off in-breeding. Because he needed to have another look at the pleading and the plan that he was sure he was going to need shortly. Unlike how it is with the other ones. Kingsley has got to be very well informed and secure in the knowledge store and the plans. That's why he was there, kneading away at them to go and read another way about the stories. Those that were stored away were in the ancient storybooks of oldies, the ones that were handed down from way back then, from in the days of glory, from the crooks to him, you know, like... Like, they were stacked away there from the old times, yes. Those were the best of times, you know, like, when the old man, his old man, was his friend. His old man would have been reigning there upon the throne as king then, and had begun to work on the plan to claim everything from all of them. For himself and his kingdom. It was the ambition of their ancestors for many generations, my e-sister. "Now, this is the time to go get it done," as seen through the eyes of this young one, e mister? Yes, yes, Siree. Damned was to be the man in the plan. Especially those of the Larried circular clan, and all those other people, too. Any and everyone who was to be found out by him, you, even. The Larrie people were then under his command and his skin. The whole Larried region now belongs to him. The young king wanted to know him now. You know, his old man, and to go ask him, where are we supposed to go and plow? What are the really important questions that we need to be getting the answer to now, like, from this point in time, and going forward? As it pertains to those things which are worth knowing, "let's go to Harvard." That right there was when and where it all started to happen. But then came...

"What! What happened?" "The bust, that's what."

12

The Windy Rushing Bust

The Wind Rush was what happened next. The squares were there, worshipping in prayer. Contented in the knowledge of the abundance of wealth they were about to acquire. Savoring the abundance of spares that were to accumulate over there that year. They were there, yes, rebuilding the square broken mess. The one-of-a-kind work that was happening all across the western ends of his address, after the flaring up of tempers, and then came the tearing down of the old dumpsters. Even more so, due to the fear of the destruction of the new buildings by some, Sir. The worried men were starting to settle in again, as the rebuilding gear neared the end. Kingsley needed to clear the air and try to pacify the people's fears again. So while they were continuing with the building, and yet more buildings that would have been happening all around Kingsley King and his kingdom's rotten end, where they were building it. They were building, yes, but they were running into nothing but more mess. Like, they were running on all cylinders, boo. Yes, man, then they started to run low on the labor plan, too. Especially cheap laborers like this one — "Who?"

"Like, like me, and you, I'm sure." Yeah, man! That's true; we were all stuck together there, and here, too, bundled up in the same old canoe. Now, tell me, can you? Anyway, look, the ship is sailing into view. Carrying much more of the same, as are the prudent things for them to do. So, they had to go looking all over, trying to find something for themselves to be sober, by seeking all around the coast to see if there were any new laborers. That's when they started looking elsewhere and looked over there. It's like this: they were looking over their shoulders bare. In looking, they saw it and shuddered. Shaking at what was about to come up and over to see the beholder they were about to clobber. They were now beholding the shouldering of all the burdens. The weight of everything came falling on him, who was leading them in carrying all the weight E-nests of the United Affairs. Yes, of all of the squares, the wares and tares, too. They were trying to fit it all in there. "True." Along with the expensive fare they knew they would have to bear, to pay for the imported labor of those who would be entrusted with upkeep and care. To keep things running and humming and keeping them always in a top-tier form, and then... It was unfair, but they were about to run headlong into Miss Fear. Whether or not the weather was to remain fair, they would surely need to confront the lady's fear. That was when they saw them. In looking over their shoulders again, yes. That was when they saw the beholder winking at them over the shoulder and remembered that they were there. Way over yonder, no wonder, my dear. "Help is over there," they said and swore not to swear, so that no sign would have had the time to get into the other guy's ear chime so they could go boasting off their mouths about what wonderful treasures they were to find, no, not this time. But it would have been because they, or someone from among them, had already known about it, you know. They knew all along that they were there, with plenty and to spare. Plenty of laborers are always willing to offer up theirs for hers. Like when they were seen offering up their labor to save her, in return for a flavor like yours, and would gladly go. For a pay-checker, you know. Like this one, who is the "Check her" personality that plays dominoes down there on the corner? Stoned, drunk, and lying in a corner, sometimes, on the other side of the town, where they'd line dance around her. Down there, where Decker lives with his wife, Miss Brown, she's the lady who wears the plaited multi-colored multi-toned greyish from a distant handkerchief on her head. And who used to go aboard and board up the broad road, "And nothing else," Hecker's words like a sword said. So, the ships would have gotten sent sailing, like... Sailing over on them there, bawling and wailing, to go and do them again. "Or, wasn't it over you and me, too? Could have been so, you know, true?"

"True."

But no, not so; luckily for us, it's not so, at least not yet. They would have gone out again, though, you bet, and wailing, yes, even though it was still hailing. Soon afterward, the hammer would have been nailing, like, nailing away at the final clip as in the Lars cough in the crooks of the army general's grip, generally speaking. His friend was there weeping, but he was there beside them and peeping, too, like peeping through the keyhole on the closed-up door in at them, and you there, sneaking in a stare. That was how we got in on the side wing and managed to see them there. All of them were there, crisscrossing the chatting before they saw him there peeping and dragged him in for a belting. Lies were lying somewhere ably. He wears long-sleeve tunics, preferably. But as for Lars and the way they are? They were not there because they wanted nothing more than something to eat and meager clothes to wear. Nothing more, and nothing less than the ice-cold beer. Nothing more than that... Well, perhaps we could ask her about the offerings of offers as were offered to them, my dear, and much more of their Sunday best to wear, yes, my friend. Like, a job, for instance, to have them go out and try to pass the test at the new age factory's address, and what for? For nothing more than to have them working the car, I guess. To keep the pothead engine a-boiling and the belly full, but we hungry bulls, going. No longer gnawing at knowing the plot that squares would have already gotten yet, but they, the circular lot, sure didn't know that. That same Square, though, the squared bearded-haired sideshow, would have gone and go... You know! Like, he would have gone way back on promises that they owe. Going backsliding to bust all the sure bets, no? "Yes." Bets that they, the Lars, had set so far, no?

"No, not this time, go."

"I thought it was so; I thought they did set those bets on the broad hoe, no?"

"No, not so."

"But, but, wasn't that the way it was before? Like, like, before they had to up and go, like. When they were seen going down to the bank where they had opted to go, yes?"

"Yes."

"I knew it all along. Man! I've got to be right even once. Like, when they went off running, trying to go and pick up the little money and come back quickly, 'quick.' Just like the man would have asked him to do with it, when last they went," so they were to have rowed. Going, going, going further on down the broad road, to the bar where they would often go to class, and took to taking the test but could not pass and, therefore, won't ever get to become a barrister's boss and get to pay back the loss before they go. Still owing their arrival here on an easy street, to some finer things that they wanted to but never did eat.

"No, you mean...?"

"No, Siree, not by their own sweet, sweaty-browed brown teeth. Tooth toot tooting the horn as is the customary norm, for much too long a day, and all night long too, no. But "gone" is coming, though. They sure don't know that humming, no, not yet. Go place a bet on it, and win; it's a sure thing.

Fast forward to the very next time they would have gotten vexed enough, messed up, and upset the settings enough, to burst out in a real sweat and rough. That was because they were not yet getting the money checks that they were hoping and wanting to get. But sweat they would have anyhow, and yet. Because squares were sitting there, still somewhat comfy in the old rocking chair. But when upon the oncoming of the comfort that was to come undone and disappeared. Complaints were setting in "scared." Where comfort's end had first begun, threats would have been seen by some as looming on. They were complaining about being wronged.

"How is it?" They were heard to wonder and spit. "How is it that we are being made to feel so uncomfortable in our own land?" There and then came those questioning commands rolling off some square tongue but directed to no particular one. They were appalled at how that was to be. What with all that imagery uploading on the stare-through for them to see? She was seeing it floating up through the eyeball, yes, booboo, Bumblebee.

"Too many Larrie brutes are out there in the quarries, my youth." So complained the complaining mouth end chute. Got to do something to clear the air in truth, to clean up the uncirculating abundance of spares and banish them all out of here. Sending them over there," look, a-pointy finger now appointed, anointed, and pointing. Showing some of them who were standing there where they needed to go, like...

"There, or there. Anywhere else but here."

Look, she's still pointing and showing it off to whoever will look. At you, even, and talking, and telling lies to haunt him, like, while still saying things like these. "I'm here showing them somewhere else to go," she said this part on the slow, yes, her, the anointed, while bowing her head in reverence at the one presiding over the ninth wing. She wanted us all to know, you know. Listen on.

"Like, out there," she further swears, "or over there, or anywhere else. Anywhere other than here. Not on our little piece of the square, no, no more." So, the call would have gone out, and out further yet. After being sent out to all of the private members' doubters, you bet. So came the scout who was heard shouting at the shouter, "Did it not come in unto them, louder?"

"Yes, it did."

"Come..." he was the one who first heard the hum that says, "Come, convene yourselves in a private chamber. We've got some things here to do and remember, these are very important things that we've got to discuss here and ponder, can't be put off any longer." So came the working wonders of the reverse, windy rushing tongues of flaming fire, as was the desire. But they did not plan it too well on the wire. So, you do know what's about to happen next, don't you, Dyer?

"Why, oh why her?"

"I don't know, but she was the closest person besides her, and the rest of them were there, so that's probably why." Anyhow. "Go up higher," he said, we've got to find new talents out there to hire, mi bred. Or else, we're surely going to fry or be left to go crying after frying the fly-fishing alone out there on the bayou. Loud and quick was to come the outcry, oh, for crying out loud, for all of it. All the complexity that was perplexing the fair city. The minority inferiority complex was to be coming in next, willy-nilly. Crying crocodile tears came from all the people who were vexed. So, heels were to be found busily taking treks; retracing those long-lost, untraceable steps back again over their necks, and then. To pacify many, they would have gone in and called them "backers." It couldn't have been made much whackier. Bet Bursc, it could not have been worse. "More work needs to be done before we go Zach-sacking them down, like money in the purse," he said. "Go on now, go, go sack those zap-heads down to the ground, grinding them ground dead."

"We've still got this." Wiseman was heard to have said he's known to have a bright crown on his head. Quite unlike some of the other well-known brain-dead. Not Wiseman, though. No one can ever accuse him of such, no. He would have stepped up to the plate and stopped the dread, you know, him. Like, like no one else. He was the only person who'd have been able to go in and talk some calm into them. That was how he'd managed to stop the dreaded fearmongering Ned. No, not the natty dread.

"Next time," he said. "The next time they leave this town, no one will know. It will take the clever hands of squares," and it did, as the way was to show.

"Go out now and show them where to go." Wiseman, it is, who was heard saying so. So, many squares went out and created a problem there where, before the times fair, there would have been none. "All Lars will be gone far away from there, by the time they're good and done. They won't know what hit them, but gone they'll be, to any other place than here by me." So said he. They would have done it all on their own free quit. Quickly quitting the willing bit. But still, they are the kind of people who were known to love a "Jill." They sure do love the jack-jobbing on low skills and having their fingers handling the fiat bills, and as for Will? Yes, William will want one of those things, still. You know, the job thing, he will be juggling and hunting around for one still. "So, here's the thing for us to do, to get their finger out of the stew. Close up shop and make them watch and not get even so much as time to chat, let alone to 'think,' wink-wink."

"No, that would be absurd; that's what I've heard. Believe here is the proper word, and since they don't ever become 'Nerds,' nor will they ever become brilliant with the sword. Just fix them up with the word, don't you ever 'think' them, just drink them; let them drink and drive the car away from here, on the way to go and get a job over there. By doing so, you would have fixed it so that some of them won't even need to quit, since they would have been dead and gone from drunk-driving sickness, Sis." While on the way out of it, you know, "it's like this," he said further. "While they're on the way, going over to some other sphere spout, trying to fend for themselves with some more workouts. They would have fallen hard upon the blown-out tires on the cars and be gone for good, no doubt. But as for this place right here? Oh no, my dear Mr. Wood. No more."

The discussion, as it was to be remembered, was highly geared at cruising speed in a private chamber. Counting the words now behind one pointy finger. Just the way he likes it to be remembered, sometimes, like, like... This time, for instance, Wiseman was to be taking his favorite instance, taking a shot at attacking his preferred better-winning dance. "What—was—it, tell me? What was that thing that would have brought them here..." He's pulling a puff on his pipe now and stroking his beard before blowing smoke in the air and continuing with their questioning song "...in the first place?" Mr. Wiseman was the one who had asked this, straight-faced. He came up with an answer before anyone else in the place, properly.

"A job!" was what Mister Wiseman heard. Turning his neck around a quarter, Bab. He locks eyes with the nerd. Wiseman it was, who had heard it and responded in turns to the sobs, as was heard. "Ugh, oh.

Right, right you are, Mister Anserley. Right, you are," and, and, answer me. What is that thing that has kept them here for all this time? Pausing again, long enough to take other puffs on the source of his brown teeth's grime. "...instead of returning 'em backside back home to the places from whence they first came?"

"A job, they still have jobs, no! Good, high-paying jobs, no?"

"You know, Sir, Mr. Anserley..." puff, they never gave you the respect properly... puff, respect you so rightly deserve. You're quite a brilliant lad! Brilliant indeed. Wow, take a nod, will you? Now, if Mr. Anserley here is correct, and the records will show that he is, you bet. What then is that thing, what is that thing that is most likely to have 'em on the next shipping plane language? Or in a training program, like a sandwich, anything. Anything at all going... puff, going out of here again?" He was pointing this question squarely at all the rest of them there, and dearly.

"Ah, a, a job, I mean, not having a job?"

The answer this time was coming from the backside of him at this point, since he was all the while turning around in his swivel chair, round and round he goes somehow. As if seeking some sort of cohesive answers out of the rest of the other dome men down the boards, while he was speaking, even, but. "Right, you're right again, Anes." Facing up to the now red-faced Ainsworth, "always-answering" Anserley.

"My dear Chap," he said. "It seems as if you're the only one around here who bothered to put on the cap, you know? Like, putting it upon the gap. You know what I mean! The thinking kind of a cap." Puff, puff, puffing.

It did seem to us as if no one else... none of the other dimwits on the conveyor belts there seemed to want in on any part of the answering tricks. They weren't getting in on the answering game bits. But then came the butting. Talking talks about nothing... but this.

"But, but." Butted in the other natty nut.

"Yes, Sir, yes, Mister Natoo Smart."

"But, we have, I mean, they, don't they have jobs? I mean. They do have jobs here, don't they? More jobs are here than there are people to fill them, as a matter of fact, no?"

"Yes, yes, Mister Smart as…, sorry, I meant to say, Mister Nattoo Smart, that's right, Sir. But things do change from time to time, don't they? Things do have a way of changing along the way. Isn't it so, Mister Smart? And that is where we, you know, people like us, that's where we come in, no?" Puffing. "You, me, and all of you honorable gentlemen sitting here by me. We are the ones who make the changes that get to happen around here. Isn't it so, Mister Knowles?" Puff.

"Yes, sir, right you are, Mister Wiseman, yes, Sir."

Mr. Knowles seemed to have known much more than the rest of the clowns around the watering holes there and crowning the town end bold… So far as it applied to his replies in answering the Wiseman's questioning, and to his seemingly uppity, upwardly altered confidence seasonings. And hence…

That wasn't to be the first time that the squares were to be doing them that much free time, you know. They'd signed in and brilliantly designed the signs of the timeless sins we'd come to own. Those types of signs were to be coming in fast, then going back out to the ports of call of the circulars in lines, perhaps. In the past, they would have used this mask, and they'll surely be coming in again in the future, not too far and fast. Squares would have been trying for a long time, in terms of years, to lie their way out of the way of pairs. Trying to avoid facing up to the never-ending tides of that long and demanding request on them and theirs. That of repairing the scars that they had inflicted, like scars that they would have inflicted upon the Lars in tricks, kids. So far, the effort has not been up to par, it would seem. It would have varied with the many tactics they had carried with them coming in, trying to wiggle themselves giggling out of the marriage. Arranging the news and re-arranging all the arrangements with Lars as it pertains to their estrangements, from the noose. Or the non-arrangements as they really were. These were the strongest of the arguments coming from her when it came to the question of them trying to shuffle themselves out of those payments, of course. The overdue repairs meant reparation: Reparation as payments, this was to be. To pay back for circular enslavement properly.

"Get over it," they were often heard to say and spit. Which meant, "Quit the whining bit, and go away," I mean, move on. Lars was to shoot right back, straight back at those pop caps in boot camp caps, and wearing their short pants, Pops. "Get over the profit you've long stuffed down into your deep pockets and pass it on." Still, no corn. Nothing seems to be happening for them in that barn. So, Lars just keeps on moving on. As it is today, Lars is seen going away, like, going, going, almost gone. But before that, the "gone" part should come along on a pushcart. Here come the plot-plotting hot spots of those squares unfairly on them from the top. They would have tried sending them back with empty pots and landed plumb on the empty-handed dumb. Failing that, stranded, um! They were to try "back in bondage." Mum, yet more some! Swallowing hard. "Oh lord!" A croak came out of the coward. Offered up a prison to keep them locked in, instead. It could have been built somewhere over there in a place called, what, something like... like L instead. For example, just for example, Mildred, we're using that sample. But "not on our shores," they were heard to have said, and trampled some more, of course. Stamping the footing as bratty children will, but still. "We'll build for you the playpen," so said most of them on the home end. "Just sign this tiny bit of paper here with my golden pen." But then again, the reply was loud and bending lower and louder. "Keep your prison, friend, we don't want it no," not nodding, like so. They were to treat and beat them cruelly. Trying hard at breaking them down, even in duels, Leigh. In a squared conception of what they'd chosen to call "A ring," a boxing thing they call it, I think, or some other such crazy sin Ting, something thing. But really now, who in the hell looks upon a four-sided square thing and calls it a ring like that cow, coward, thing? Really? E Neily! But still, nothing is being done for them, it would seem. Nothing except for that said swinging ring thing that they're in, the boxing thing. Among a few other such schemings. They back him up and lock him in. In this boxing ring sin ting, something. Boxing him in, and his head, too, with him. Beating him around as if he were a clown, the circular being as he was known. But it was not to be just him, alone. Anything that they could get their claws on, to relieve them of their living space, was all gone. Leave him weakened, even when he was winning. Outwitted, belittled, disgruntled, and dispirited. Throw him in there along with the rest of them, barefoot, Ed. Toss them all into the pen again and lock them in there. Gave them what they did not ask for (beer) and sowed discord among men. Pile on crooked laws and criminal records, then pick them up again upon trumped-up charges. Pack them in on a plane bound back to the yard as is, and then. Again, the outcry was loud and harsh. Plain and clear, they were forced to hear the backlash. "Of your doing, squared face, you had better beware." Running scared again. Time for them to step up their game. So, the squares were to have gone about changing and shaking things up quite a bit, sup... around the place; no expense was spared. No stone was left unturnedover, over there. They were to come crawling upon the wildest, weirdest ideas and offers that one could ever have plunged the hearing aid under the best. One offer after the other. Then they tried to pass those "after" offers off to unsuspecting partner staff. Governing governors and wannabe leaders, too, since you'd asked. Those coming from the countries of (by then) common poverty, and becoming even povertier than you and me. Filing in from other parts and regions of the world too, wherever Larrie's feet had dared to stand, or go walk their own shoe where such people as ours came from? Mostly the Larry kind of people them, *yuh nu-hoe dem? yardie sin ting aggen.* But not just us and them, no. They did it unto some other people too, some from among their friends, who, did you ask? I'll tell this as a fact, from among those squared selves, even. Speaking of yardie in the yards, all I had to do was summon up the guardie, yes, the guards. Like, like that one, the mister man whom they called bodyguard, and it's because. "I wouldn't like your job," as they had said. I beg your pardon. Oh, I mean, you're my pardy, partner. *Yes -mi bredda* man.

Yeah, man, remember, a Jamaica yaad mi come fram, sorry, I meant to say; I'm Jamaican born and bred, okay? Yes, wordplay is the order of the day around here. So.

Squares were (over many years) doing those sorts of things over there. Doing it as if to try and reposition themselves for the big move, like. The movement of the squares up to the meeting in the spheres, so. He had to go back to sitting on his school stools. Creating new tools for old fools. Tools of his trade are now these, as they apply to the squares in need: Bills of wronging the right side of whatever one might have lied or lie around with. Like, a bright shining light, rightly or wrongly set, coming in to get you and take you to bed, as already said. "Sheets." Setting it firmly and tight against the wrong, Mister Wong, that's it, yes, run along. Then go two blocks down and turn right at the first traffic light to find out which way they're going to practice tonight, to try and learn how to do the cop vice. It's the custom over there, overnights, where they go to their former farms to charter a billing building. That is to be the building block "A." Go see it. That's a must for you, Bey, *yuh sei mi?* Yeah. Since we've got to take a bus to go back up the eleventh step and to get to Constitution Hill, where they are, even now, still framing the treaties that are to be hung on the doorstep sweetly, ee? Yes, still, and drafting the bills of laws and rights, as they're there even now, this very moment in the night. Putting in more orders, ordering yet more bills that will soon be coming in, as they were ordered from further away. But yet undelivered and coming in from the cold, where they were plucked and packaged in boxes coming off those old wild birds. Those who are out there singing sweetly under the Treaty trees, so I've heard, sweet Leigh, and much more than before, are things like these. But seriously, though, did you even know? Did you know that is how such things go? That's the groove right there, among other designing gears. They're all designed to get you moving and gone, out of here. He would have been busying himself pushing Lars deep into a tight car. Cornering them too, on all that tasty brewed beer of theirs, and har, I mean, hers. Putting in the calls of the bulls and the bears, all on a pair of scars off the market. By making life hard and living even harder for the half-wits, and making criminals out of decent, hardworking people, partners like this, and out of those other gals, my girls. Everybody knew it already. Anybody grumbling? "Loudly." Did anyone know what the real deal was with what was happening at the club, or how to stop it from happening to the one I'd loved? "Hardly." Well, no one other than those, the squared ones, pardon me, I'd supposed that they knew. But as for them stopping it from happening to you, and the half-wits? No, that sort, they wouldn't do. Because it wasn't the habit of those with the magic to go on and stab it in the foot of the rabbit, then shove it down the pit. Things were happening just like they'd wanted them to... Or more like, just as they had planned them. So that they may go out (or come right on in) and make yet bigger fools out of all of them. Out of those Lars folks, even. Even went so far as to kill some, mad some, and burn some. Born some, deformed some, reform some. Inform some, run some, convict some, and un-dick sum... This type would have been happening regularly upon the gypsum, and yet more "some" were waiting in the wings and longing to come. Then, when all that summing up of the "some" sums was all good and done. That was when he was to offer up a brand-new prison. But for the safekeeping of the remaining gnomes' combs who would be leaving... soon. Plus a few measly pound bumps bumped upon the pound sums. But that fire did not catch on, so they had to go back to the scratch pan. That's what led them to the no-plan sack scam. "Just pack them up and send them home with nothing on, nothing more than a covering gown to put a foot down, or six." No mention of them ever paying up for, like, the pension plan for which they'd long worked hard, yikes! Like this. Can't afford, no, can't follow them home back to the yard. "Oh, my Lord!" The outcry was hard, and loud was the G-string musical chord. "Got to go back now to the drawing board," said the kingly word of their lord. "Brother, bring out the hits," he was heard saying on a spit. "Go, show them the way out of the exit. I can't do any more than this; I quit. It's up to you now; go on. Get them out of here and quickly through the door jamb, get them gone. Go on now and do it, go get it done quickly. Just in case someone fires up the lit... Leigh." That was it; breathing was to come next, teething through the exit. That was to be the next trick. And now, this is it. No, I can't explain such a feeling. Watch out now for more double dealings.

13

Postings on the Squares

Meanwhile, there were similar postings over there, on the other side of the squares' outer divide, I hear. The other squares were busy on the inside row, busily devising those schemes and plans of theirs, you know.

"Oh no."

"Yes, yes, my dear. Oh yes, my dear child." They were busy too, like. Busying themselves up to go and fix the Lars' business, boo, and yet other bits and pieces of an old jogging shoe. Due to his desire to go and fix them up good and proper. In some more goods and property tax matters, such as those that were coming from the actors leading the pack is stand out at mixing up, yet the more, Papa, and... and...

"And what, man, the mix-up music of maxed-out credit cards mastered out and called in?"

"Yeah, man, that one, you're extra hard-in, airy." Way before the day should come for the exit that you're on, even." Even after the Brexit bricks were packed together, on the concrete mixture the master mason had poured out, on the bredda. Oh yes, my brother. Fitting it securely into the pocket fillings and rendering it all kicking in. But as for Lars, blind and clueless as they are, they were there busily resisting him or mixing in with the trick sin thing, sometimes, Mister Mistar. The quick fixes of all those schemes and plans, as fine as those are, aren't mine. But all those plans were so designed as to see them gone from under his star. So now, look. Gone they are, Will, look at them. They're going down Daniel Boulevard still. They're still going now, look at them, going, going, slowing yes, but going, not quite yet gone though. Not by their own free will of thorn, no. Because there are posts over yonder that need to be filled, and the boats are sailing in, still. But as for those who are going away, listen up now to what they have to say: Now, off we go, Gore, just as we would have done oftentimes before, much, much more. Like, like, remember when hahaha, remember when, like, when at first, we had to pack up the shop and leave the store? Remember! Hahaha. That was something, ee, mass Vin! Wasn't it, Sir? And, when we had to pull up the stakes and go, I mean, come over, to this very spot even, which is... "It's, it's, it's not that hot no more though," she said this on a dying sob, getting yet slower, slow. "So sad." That's sad, sniff, sniff. Look, tears are now shed over it. Wipe, wipe, wipe it away now. Oh sheet! But, back now to the talking score; yonder far, there's a place that I know my star. She continued saying, when she said this to Har, I meant to say her. To her. A place that is happening, milk and honey flowing in from afar. Fools only will stay away, even fooler fools than those will tarry here, but as for me, I must go over there, I'm out of here before this whole shipwreck gets overthrown on them sitting on the board-up game and set the boat blazing off on a row. But what they, the Lars, did not know was that they, just as always, never knew how anything goes, ever, and so... Now, let's just take hold of our listening earlobe and go on in there. Just to see if we can get a stare "ring wheel" in there and get to hear how the squares are going to fare. Now that they're all gone. Those Lars would have left the barns and gone out of there, you know. Servant class, they are and were, and always will be. That's for sure, just like me. But now, listen up. This is how it was about to go. "Not on our squared shores," they were heard to have snored. No, no more space is here for them on our floor since they're no longer ours.

"Who then, who's going to balance out the score for us?" asks another one more, of the tugs. Much more so than before, those questions were floating through the door and soiling the rugs. Because Lars would have grabbed the first airplane... the thing they could find going out in the line. Then came the next training center engine, motoring eight cylinders, trailing the trained engineers in, in kind. Like motoring them around on the motor ring for the production line. All kinds of transporters were coming in at that time, in a like manner. Just to then turn around and go out again, carrying a lot more of them and their mama, away, crying. Like kicking and screaming, too. Look at them going, running even, into you. Woo! Trying to get through this thing that I'm viewing, you. There they are, going, going, gone away. Yeah, man. Gone are they, just like the real Lars, I'd say. Hopped onto the streetcar or on any other cars that might have been going their way. The train even had to turn the engine around and go again in the same direction from whence it came that evening, down. Laden heavily with Larried Lars's legacy, along with their nervously wrecked families, running away from all the agony, agony agony agony, ee man? Yes, and the miseries too, probably. Perceived, even though it might have been made out to be over there in the kingdom of squares' broken, as in promises due. Unto them, and you, in their dreams, and yes, yours, too. But "there's another place over there," so I was to hear them swear, a place that's not too far away from squares. "That's where we're going next, my dear. Heard that it's really 'happening,' and laborers are lacking. That's my kind of sacking setting in right there." So said some of them there, in our hearing gear, even. "In no time, I'll be up and running again."

"Well, of course," said another one of us and ours. Yes, you'll be running. Like, such running as, off to a work refrain, and refraining from playing pay-checkers games. Which will be gone long before it's gotten "get" again anyway. Running off to stores and shopping at yet more malls, I'd say. Buying things that are posted on everything, like stalls, is okay. "Yeah?" "Yes." Because that's what money is good to fall for, and that is all, yes, my star. Yes, yes, Mister Mister. Squares are still there, though. Watching those Lars as they go, leaving the place bare. Veering sideways from the familiar airflow, while wearing a pain-painted, faint frown on the regular stare through. "What is going to become of them there, though?" The look-backing Lars was heard saying to have cared. "Oh!" Yes. But they're not Lars' business anyway, not anymore.

Even more so now than before, because Lars' car is gone, they've moved on. He's got to get moving along, too. Now they're altogether gone, all of them, and you. None of them left around here to remain. Look at them, moving along, swinging the linked-up arms, and singing the happy swan songs. "Deliverance has finally come." But, back over there, though, like, there where they were running away from the door, near the hut. Oh, look! They're leaving the sulking squares a-looking on as if in a rut. The sulking stares will soon be gone, no doubt. That gone, has already begun to burst out into a happy dance. As in "them," singing with the strums of the sing-along songs, look! Look at them. They're out of their houses and running into the streets even now, mere minutes after the Lars were to skip the town once more. They're there singing songs of another kind of merry cow. Or more like a song about marrying, that's how. Marrying off the merry-making, and making it last only so long that they, the Lars. They won't ever want to come back here, nor care for the calves. "So long, Larry," said the wrong lady, "thank you for the curry, I mean, carry." Well, yes, that too, you know. Like, the curry and you. But more so the carry than the curry. For the carrying in of all of it, those good and godly things that you would have brought in towards our profit. Did you not carry the wealth of the world over here to give to us? Like, to give it to me, and him, to all of us, to live in? Then, gone you are, there you go. Look at you, going the way to go and leave, and even with mirth and glee. Happy are we, though you will not get to see it yet. Busted bet. Look at them, Squares are now really sitting up there on almost all that the world has got to spare and spend. They can feign remorse now for how things would have turned out in their interest there, wow, for as long as doubt may be upon the mouth of anyone, and everyone. Even on the limp hanging shoulders of the manikin family man. Everyone around those places out there on the line in the lime green. All of them over there on the golfing greens, even. See what I mean, Steven? Because when Lars stood up and left the scouts. Leaving those Squared shores, they went out and about, then proceeded to get out of their houses and go see about their route out. They were leaving behind them: The set goal, and all that gold — "No, don't shout it out!" Ssshheee...! Shut your mouth, don't tell a soul. Tell it to no one and his breakfast bowl, of all those gold and silver, diamonds in the sty-man. Had to hide them somewhere where the eyes of the I-man would not even suspect looking, nor get a feel for the finer things to cook in... Which is good for healing, as is written in the Book of Facts. To the soul, even, yes, that's the hook, don't talk. But go on now, go on over there and hide them in. Like, go hide them in there among the other hidden things of the Squares that I'm in, you know. Like, out there where all those others are, still hiding, even now. In the mud pen and mingling with all those sows, near the hens. But won't be for much longer than now, surely not forever, and ever. Amen.

...

Meeting of the minds. Over there on the square, there was a call that was heard coming upon the hearing chords of all those Squares, coming home to them from him and his kind, kingly square. Young Kingsley had to open the eyes of the blind. After all, their helpers had just skipped the town and gone, so... "Stop the whining, my brother," he said, "You're not the other, you're mine." So said Kingsley King, Divine. Now, this would have been several Kingsley Kings later on down the line. But the same saving scenario had (obviously) come back to haunt them in his time. "Look, look out there at the fields," Kingsley IV was heard saying to those eels. "Look at the fields, they're bursting with wine. It can all be ours, brothers, both yours and mine. Have you got a longing, my brother? Haven't we got the power here? Let's get up now and go on over and actualize the slaughter. The sharing shall come after." Laughter, and yet more laughing laughter. But then came the ring. "Schering," comes the death-sounding, stung ring from the sword unsheathed. Nephew wanted to be mentioned in the planting of the seeds. In the planning, too, and in the drafting of the reasons why you... He was akin to the Stevens, the Bungie one, even. Retracing steps now backward and faster was what we heard coming in after the aborted laughter. The nephew was smarter than they had at first bargained. He wanted rules to be drawn up faster and agreed upon before all drawn swords could be laid back down. So, back to the drawing of the board game went the crown. To see about the crafting of the draft that was then drawn up and handed down there as... I mean, as they were asked. Upon the agreed sharing criteria, task name, even, and then. With the shaking of hands, it was all good and done for them. So came the end to the feared start of war again, between men who are friends. It would have been a real shame if it were to happen to them that way, but... How did such a thing come about, you'd asked? These are the facts, Mr. Wood, my boss. Kingsley Kings would have gotten himself dragged into the acts of the family way with them and him, you know, and hence. This was what would have softened the edges of the Stevens' den. That's how Bungie's nephew was to find himself sitting there amongst those men in view, instead of me and you. To be found numbered with them there. However, he knew full well that it was his uncle — "You mean, that belated Bungie bundle?"

"Yes. Yes, it was he, him." It was the Bungie one himself, not me, I'm not a king. It was he who'd caused them to become anything with wealth, and not to have been humbled like all the rest of us, and she on the shelf. Now they seem to think that it's okay for them to go and write him out of the way. "No way," I heard him say.

Bungie's brothers would have built a house upon what each of them would have learned the most. They went out on the roads and prospered. Therefore, they reigned alongside the many kings ever after, serving and being served by the heathens and paupers. Being counted as building blocks of the Kingsley king times, unto this time even. Down the Royal lines to the nerds, in the evenings. But as for you, and yes, him too, this is what I've heard them say to be true. Designer lifestyle and the worthless mess he packages and sells to you, and guess who? Yes, you know the truth. You bought into the nothingness, nothing new. Woo.

The problem, as it was to be seen there on that memorable day, though, was like this; this time, even though it was to be according to the plan that the squares would be taking the fight against every other human, everywhere, in lines. It was about to start among them and then move on to the neighbor on the border. Same as how things were in the days of the former. And then, as I heard it said that day by some of their friends. They were going to be wiping out the outsiders. Be it from among themselves or wider, as was supposed to be the case at this pivotal point in the existential race. "Or all of them even," said the same Kingsley, the thieving... "But only if need be." As it is in this case, of the seasonal herb tea, there was nothing but needs to beat, so... "If you're not in on this with us," said the king, as they were to hear him say it in a cuss while laughing with them, not us. "Then you are out and are to be numbered with the dust." That was the beginning of "The end" for all of those who were found to be among the side called "them." Which might somehow turn out to include folks like us, beware... of them. It was to be a war to end all wars, said those men and friends over there, and most worthy a cause. But then again. Those "them", as they were to find out later on, were found to be not such an "easy" a going-away kind of thing, as I. They would have won for themselves some valuable things in the warring field, to see. Things such as another chance at going on, and at living, on fees. If only for another day, or season, and living was what they did, yay. But everyone already knew that that was not how it should go, and time alone was going to show what next would be the next route squares would take, to get them to leave and go.

The hopes of a Lar. Now and then, there comes such a person. Someone whom they refer to as a Sesom. This entity is one that was found to be equipped with the ability to dream dreams and to see visions. Such a person, they say, has the potential for Larrie liberty and freedom, okay? "Yeah." But it never came running over to them on the weed run, no. Those grandiose dreams are yet to be seen; they usually seem to just wither and die there in the seams. Those dreams that, (without fail) seemed to sail to them and us from land, leading squarely back to the toenails of the squares. Squares who would have been sitting somewhere out there on a crooked electric boogie chair and firing bullets point-blank into the spheres of Lars' curly locks of hair. But doing so from behind the walls of a closed-up jail cell. Somewhere where no one can ever see anything from the outside, oh hell! Not anything at all that may be going on within on the inside, and, therefore, nobody on the outside would be able to go and tell it to anyone else. So, no one ever gets to tell the true stories of how Sesom, in all his glory, had stumbled and fallen headlong into the very hellhole where some squares were sitting in the Squares' doorway. Those very squares who had once sworn upon beer that that is where all "Sesoms" from the Larrie's doldrums are going to find the freedom forged in their wise wiz dumb. The Lars' kingdom will never come, it would have seemed. Not until, and unless he learns how to get up off that thing, and go get it done with his own two hands in a team. Instead of sitting there and waiting for the other "someone" person to come back, bringing in the sheaves to give them to him, in a sack. "Power is not given," so they say, it is always taken away. That's the total cost of the sum to split, okay? Or is it? That's the question to knit, but. Oh, sheet, look at this. No, don't do that, don't cuss a lot, that will get you nothing but biting the dust in that slot. Because, to them, you're nothing more than an excess load that must be shed, like Sheddy the dragon, who was proud to be standing out there in such a distinguished crowd on the said night mi bred, looking. Look, they're gathered there. Majoring in leaving you out of everything there, just as much as out of everything else down here, and dead. Or more like, leaving you in at least one thing, like, in there. You know the song, now, sing it in my ear: in *dey Jah Jah, Jah Jah in dey*. The year of the pale horse is what it is, it could easily be said, after the oftentimes when they'd be seen there weaving the webs with twines and wielding their swords at leaving you dead. Yes, every decision, every law. Every purpose and every cause leads them one step closer to applause. After they're done with spoiling you and giving you over to the grave clothes boiling cavity, grazing in the grass yard mi dread natty, yardman style ee. Boiling out there in the hot Sandy gully, "That's such beautiful scenery," look. You know! Nothing one may say here will halt the situation over there, I swear. They will more easily go out and halt the speaking tongue station from the inter-

fare... aunts. That's because, according to them, you're spoiling the fun that the man and his sons had planned to come down on you, at once. Just like they have been doing, when doing the other plans, and the dodos, one shoe is in... Even as they've already done to me and you. Happened when they did it to all the other men who would have dared to rise with the morning sun and get a standard tan, burning the melanin in the tanning canoe, but tell me. Can you?

"No."

"I know." That's just the luck of some lucky ducklings who would have fallen on the draw of the sword and shook-shake the edges while shaving the dust off the word so that it may go on down. A-boogie on down, on down. Boogie on down.

Meanwhile, they sent you out in style, while covering up your bones in foolproof snake oil, and... Gave my mother two guesses to try and tell me what the sex of my roommate is. But you know, Mom, she's very unlucky like that one, and this, of course. She was wrong, both times, equally.

14

The Roll Call

In total, this roll call was like calling Bungie's entire family in. It was for this very reason that he would have labored and even lived. "As of now," said Kingsley to you on the plow, and he, yes, him. But surely not to me, I wasn't looking, that's my only reason for escaping. "From now on," he said, everything in the enemy's hand shall be something that we would have planned, produced, and passed on down as something to eat and bickle fei nyam, as foods. But, in fact, it will be a weapon of mass destruction in the enemy's own hands. Who's that? You'd asked, go back over there and sit on your asked… question. You'll soon find out the reason for the injection. "New forms of weaponry must be given to the army," he said, "which won't even look like armor in an army. Not in the conventional words of usury, no mi bred." This is to continue until the job is done properly. So, go on now, go out and call them. Call in all the artisans and skilled visionary men, those who will commit themselves to the greatness necessary to see the proper outcome in the end, and those who will be willing and ready to go out and get it done. All the researchers and scientists, like that one over there, and this. Manufacturers, lawmakers, money changers, and others.

"Like whom?" you'd asked the man and his brothers standing by you in the room.

"Them," he pointed out, in his reply. He shoved his pointy finger so close that it almost stuck them in the eye. Yes, them and theirs, not you. Those who are cunning at manipulating borrowers, we need them all in our corner to get them to go out and become bigger borrowers than

Mr. Warner, you know. Like, let them go out and borrow other people's money, our money, to go out and buy large stockpiles of nothing (that's so funny). So that we may get them to come running back regularly, paying us back with everything that they've got willy-nilly, and more. Then continue doing so, until what's left of their meager life is over. We've got a cause that is greater here, and great is to be the partakers in the stakes to share on that day when everything shall be taken away from them, all of them there. From all of those "other" guys' stake, and from those haters who bake for us the cake, and shall become ours altogether, to take. That day is now at our door. So, go ahead and have your fun world, cause don't you know, they're wielding death at new swords. Go ahead... Oh, hell no, that will be all that is going to fall on this stall, to protect ourselves and prevent infringement calls. The outcry was again loud and clear, children. But coming through the Circular walls as something to thrill them. More calls were to come falling upon the ears of the other squares, too. Those who weren't in the mode of marching the troops down the road to kill them, yet, and you. Or even up to the heavy load to refill them on booze, who knew? They wanted to go in and get what was left of the head-top above the other guys' neck, in the end slot, but what the heck! The rest of the world was battle-weary and would not allow it to continue, in theory. No, they were not going to be joining in it this time to go riding along with them on their war-frontal views, if I'm not lying. But Kingsley's squares didn't bother to argue. Arguing is what Lars does, and continues to do. There are others, too, like those who will be gone far from view. When all is said and done, there will be nobody's bone no. No such bones at all will be left around to argue, Kingsley knew that much about the hour of truth. The rest of them won't know what hit them by the time the squares are done with hitting them with their boots, and you? "So, the conventional weapons of warfare are gone from the squares' scarred spheres." Kingsley King was heard telling those square scars there. "Well, not totally gone, but we're laying them down now. We've already laid them away, huh, wow. Well-preserved and stashed away somewhere in town, okay?" Just in case we should be called upon to take them up again before this new phase settles in properly, to fade them away. But don't forget the nuclear and other weapons of mass destruction. Those are most handy to have on a man's right hand, as is the custom, just in case there should again come a need for them. But as of now, here's how and with what our battles shall be fought and won, children. How our lessons are taught to the lesser ones and learned, to kill them. Lessons that shall bring us victory before their eyes even get to turn and see any of it. So, the tools of the trade are now these, as they apply to the squares in need. These tools are made for fools to tease and are great to meet up with our mighty men's deeds, like: Scientists and technics, yeah! Yes, Siree. Technicians are these. Those who will be going out soon, and, instead of building deadly bombs to blow up in a mighty blast, and sound off an alarm that will attract their attention fast. At the risk of invoking their ire, stir them into action, and fire them up to rasp... Those who will then do things as if to slow us down and tire us out. Here's what we'll do, no doubt. Go instead into the lab, and put on your white gowns, Fab... Go in and create things as you're accustomed to fabricating, go make a mess that will further our cause down west towards their gates and gaping... holes. Like, from this point on and down the line, be bold. Chart a path for a human civilization that enables good living on a healthy plantation. In other words, right here on the planet that can support only a much smaller and truly sustainable Hugh, man, pop Hugh lay shunned. One that will see us (just us) living in it, from then on. Like, by us for us, alone. Home. And so it was, from then on down. They set out from there and began going about the stated task of messaging them up and down the stairs. Doing them in on the mess, but not that alone, no. Beware. With dressed-up death, too, and destruction as a jet-set, true. To show off to them and you. Then set them in on the most sophisticated styles and fashion quests, "yes?"

"True, true."

Then they sell it to me and you, under modern societal views, and you, I mean, "we." Yes, that would be us, we bought into it with money that we could not afford to fit in our cut of the non-profit shoe stews, on the bus. Yeah, man, the man was killing us slowly and softly with his song, Food, and water. Gangs stirred booze and medical disaster. Sick care, hardware, software, and softer... Birth controller and mutant jeans ore... This thing here, and that one over there. Laws and customs and things to wear, upon the butt some even, over there. "Where?" There, where there's a needle hole after the injection, I swear. Yeah, even there. More news and information on the tell-lie vision. Sickness and diseases, the most dangerous diseases. The list is long and continues to grow, along... Yet more tools for fools were to be tossed into the pools on the commons. So now, here for you are some more of those tools to please, yes, some such as these: Like, like, shaking the spear in front of his spheres, because Lars was known to be always copying squares, in anything and everything, and everywhere. Wearing whatever pretty little things that might be there to wear and going nowhere. Crafting it all in on them and their half-springs, like catching the mice, flying the trap baited with cheese, always shunning the lights, off him. It's the custom of those squares over there, overnights, be advised. Then there are those "Charters" again that they are after, to rightly gain the rights to start the Bill of Rights offers. By building up the buildings, yes, the right billing buildings. Much more so than before are things like these in the store. Stars in magazines are in the news on TV, with social media reports, coming in weekly. But seriously, though, did you even know? Did you know that that is how things go? "Psychotherapy for thee," so said he. What they see, what they hear, and even the very clothes they wear. All shall be weaponized to get them gone and out of here. Inflammatory agenda of the media. Manipulating people into a frenzy is the idea. Selective reporting, wicked pedio... This is what they're scouting to do to you: a weed whacker. With the Iddie hat, you love to wear so much. The rod of correction is gone from your parents' hands, and so, too, are your children, Mom. Child "sexy" tradeoffs and on, the police, man-on-man violent crime in the streets. The inept tick slouch is what your leaders are all about. Pretentious know-it-alls know nothing enough to halt the people's stalls, shout yes!

"Hallelujah!"

"Well, you're fairly and wonderfully blessed, I guess, Sister Julia." Murderous plots and conspiracy theories. Vaccine, drug addiction, and TV series. Emotional manipulation of the masses. Manipulating the psychology of the people. Taxes. Especially to the young, their media sells dumb, to lay them down, and lies to feed. Shows them what to need that their papa should never read, nor do a breath test over to keep them sober. All this is happening while you're slowly being rolled over the edge, even to the deathbed, hammering away with the per c sledge, yes, em C hammer. Like, to the no-longer-to-be-here ever-after, land. Scares the living daylights out of you, and the golden sunshine out of the morning dew. If you should ever dare to do what they don't want you to do, and when you do, the other things too. But then again, who knew?

...

How was the ball game? I heard them asking the squeegee boy with the small name. He was watching the ball game on TV some time ago. A baseball game it was, to show the facts. It was a very close match, tension was running batch, like it was that high. A very astute and capable hitter was at the plate to bat. "Why?" Because of a loaded base ahead of him at that. If one remembers well the thing to whack, the pitcher, yes, look at him. The pitcher would have tried everything to get out of the inning with the least damage (if any at all) done to him. He would have thrown one ball after another. But like, straight, at the hitting hitman of a hitter. Or something more like: straight at his head, bitter. Each time getting closer to hitting the person instead of striking and worsening, you know what I mean, like, striking and worsening him out. Each time, the hitter would stare down the pitcher while shaking his head in disapproval, as shown to the spitter. Or like, just to say, without saying it as it is known in a down-home way, "Hey! Don't do that, okay?" Try to hit the bat or miss it if you want to score a strike with a whack. But one pitch after the other would have inched in a little bit closer, until... He would have walked the hitter over the hill. With one of the closest misses yet, you bet. Or was it a slight nick on the helmet? Seems that close to a snitch who is here now chatting about this. Anyway, the hitter ran hard and fast, and down on the pitcher at last, instead of trying to get to the base quicker to score a pass. He ran down on the pitcher and whacked him hard over the head, thick, thicker... "Yeah!" Yes, with his helmet, mister. All hell would have broken loose. All because of that moose, oh, look at him go. The point one is trying to get at here is this. If the man is out there telling you in no uncertain terms how to kiss, up. Telling you that the things that you're doing are not okay, and are the cause of some concerns, ugh. Not good at all, not for anybody. Including you and his daddy. But you will not listen because your head is tough, the water is muddy, and the seas are rough. Then, it might at some point in time become really necessary for one to open up that tough thing a bit. Or at the very least, test it and see just how tough it is, or is going to be. Hence, if we're all being told to curb and control our actions because the earth is in a grave crisis, or even a fraction of an overpopulation vice-grip. And everybody needs to play a part in tackling the problematic spoiled rice mix. And he, that man over there with the key. No, not me, but that one across from you. He's the one who has got the power and the real threatening stare. Real powerful hardware too, to go along with it, mixing, and adding it into the other wares, warring with you, even, to go further with the pair. As you already know fully well, he's the one who can and does anything he feels like doing to anyone; everyone knows it too, even you, as said before. He tells you in plain language what you can and cannot do. Tells you what you should, as well as what you should never do. He's telling you indirectly even now, via the laws, vows, customs, and norms. All new and alien are these to you, me, and our moms, and we wonder why the guy is doing and saying these things through his palms, please. But he lied. To hide his true, shapely, and colorful pride.

Meanwhile, the very few of us who are thinkers amongst you on the bus. We know, and we would have been trying hard to point it out to you as we went along the road to go through towards Porus. But you screw and unscrew the bottled brew, the face even. While continuing, as usual, you and the gal dem, as school gal, you know. Girls, girls everywhere, I swear. If in the process of doing all of the do-dos that you're long known to be doing.

"On the home end?"

"Oh, yes, I'm talking to you, one shoe in?"

"Yes, I know, but who told you so?" Oh, I see! If, in the process of doing so, you were to threaten to undo all of the work that the man and his sons had done. On you, even, on the earth's equilibrium, and order. Or just on his survival customs, on the borders. How long do you think it's going to be before that man and his children, or someone else with his blessings and his permission, to "kill them," are going to whack you hard over the whole yard of your very hard, deadhead, charred, and messy? Or even worse, like, over your whole nation or continent, nurse? Well, I'm just guessing this verse. This, especially if and when you and everyone else know full well that he, not only can, but will. Come on. *Cum unda de sin Ting nuh man*, you know, like. Get under the stand, where you might begin to get understanding and start to stand up firm on your own feet and land "ding," on your toes, or even on your two hands, ten fingers licking the dripping fat off the cocoa. Since feeling the feet doesn't seem to do it for you, doing it under the stand, Hingh Sheeves, might. Don't do it, my youth. "True?"

"True."

But then again. One might be tempted to fire back something at him and ask. "How is it that you've come to love other people's children so very much, and so fast, King, as you're asked? So much so that you will give up on yours so that the other man's children may live and last, and prosper ever after him?" So, he says to you: sign this pledge here, Boo-boo, the pledge that I, you know. My kind and I would have sat down this time and thought it up, and had it all done. Then drew this draft and firmed it up for you, lump sum. This is a pledge for you to sign and agree to, Boo-boo. So that I may continue to control, govern, and tell you what to do. Just like I've always done to you and all others like you. Even without your input, without getting your permission. Or even a contribution from anyone, such as you, to the said plan while we were there, rendering it... Yes, this very plan that I'm now giving towards your living, even... eat it, eat it. Even though you did not know what was going on while it was being done, last evening. But now, I'm giving it to you, and I'm telling you to agree with me to sign this decree to have no baby pickney. "My children," he said, "listen to me. No more." Or, just one, if there must be, oh, you poor... But no more than two, certainly not three. Didn't you agree and sign the petition decree? Yes, yes, you did. Because, as you can see, the Earth is over, p. As in, overpopulated. As you already know, some men are undervalued and low-rated. And "we," we must do something to save the earth for the future, and for "our" children's worth. Look at her, cute ee!

"Yes, she's cuter."

Who are those "we," whose children are those supposed to be? Now, hear me if you can, Bee. You will have neither of them, you know. Those two children that you wanted so very much to rent, to own. Because you've just signed their testament, the dump yard treatment for your children's feet is mint, yes, I see the icy mint. That same one solution to a planet-saving scheme of which she speaks? For whom was it meant, to your descendants, sent? No further arguments.

Did you even know, though? Did it ever occur to you that's what men like him do to follow through on the generational extending view through this slot? But as for you, what do you do? You go right on out and do what the other man tells you to. So, when he's there telling you that this Kingsland earth is already through with supporting me and you. It can support only one, so to speak, that man, well, so said that one-of-a-kind, man of the week. But if there are still many men standing thereupon the planetarium, and far too weak. Much more than just that one, like, those who are real men from the clan. "Oh! Um..." Maybe not, but men who have all found a stance upon which to stand, like, on the overpopulation program, yes? "Yes." Let's say, they're already there standing, or have been there last evening, adding their little piece of action to the plan, while we were all sleeping, no? "Yes, I, I must get my rest." "I know, but..." But that man is the one who is there leading the planning of the plan, right? He's among the few still left standing upon that stance, and bright, right?

"Right."

How likely, then, is the fan to take off with that man and his friends, leaving another one standing up in the stands at the end? Just one, you know, out of all of the other ones. That would have been after all the rest were already gone, you know, like, all of the excess ones, such as would have been so decided upon by those very men. They would have all been gone by now and moving on, no? Since they're of the lesser brotherly flow, they're gone. No? Leaving just those who are strong and the earth can sustainably support, only them, right?

"Right."

But then. You turn your head around and are about to see that you're that, like, that one man remaining on the earth still standing and strong, right? Wrong. Go sing another song.

15

Imagined Nation

"What is this?" he asked. "Is this all in my imagined nation? Or not?" Well.

"We are here," they were heard to have said and swore when they were swearing... "We are here because you were there." They were heard shouting this out rear, even as recently as last year. Shouting it out there in the spheres of those squares. Not knowing, it would seem, that, as for him and his kind, like those square men and their kings in their lines. That's what they were there fighting for, too, for themselves, or more like fighting against. They were out there fighting against having to have the likes of you and those others, including him, that one, and his brothers. Oh yeah! I know, that means me, too, yes, man. They were there fighting against having the likes of us hanging around out there on their square fence. With nothing to do other than to smoke out the sweet honeybees and curse with our mouths at them, it makes no sense. They were busy there, making themselves look busy. Pushing them, and the likes of them, and everyone else who may have been looking for anything the likes of them, out of there, Biz, Inez. But they thought that it was they who were there doing the push-backing. Bushing the bulls... again, and weed whacking. They were pushing back at those squares, trying to get them to do more giveaways, to them and their... by giving it to them on Friday evenings. So that they may continue to go on living that way. Trying to make a living each day on the little morsel that they were being given as pay. Like, they were trying to get those squares to give yet more money to those "lazy good-for-nothing, not-going-a-good-way people." As they are looked upon and seen by those from the other vehicles, even now. Those who were there praying, though, and doing the Thanksgiving servicing calls, like so. Calling it a blessing and payments to them from you know who... Or more like: payments that were long due, and overdue; owed to them, him, and you. They would have surrendered this small thing to do, who knew? They had forgotten; it would have seemed to those of us in the wee group that I'm in, often. They'd forgotten to accommodate such things in the asking scheme. They'd forgotten to ask about some other things that were due to them. Such things as "repatriation is a must, I know." Now, let's get off the bus and go. "Oh, wait a minute, no," so said another mother of a fah fah far away, father. That might not be such a good idea. It might turn out to be a mistake, they say, to my Nadia. No man, no. That might not be so good in the long run, so let's stay on, look, man, let's stay here and bet on whatever little we can get in the belly here, via the long tongue. Knock-knock, knocking upon the bang gut while drinking beer; quack-quack, down. Like, like, things to eat and wear. Better a little bit than none, like, nothing at all. Like, let's opt for a slightly better pay package, she meant, to go and buy mint balls and sausage for two cents. But nothing about the repair was soberly meant, no such thing at all. Over-due payments, too, as long as the over-the-shoulder water boot kind of shoe was the tallest one for the oversized repairmen, who were seen com-ing through to me. Yes, that should include you, and yet others such as them, those from over there in Back-to. See?

"Yes."

Everything else but them paying us back for other services rendered, and labor already tendered. While they were (seemingly) forgetting to ask about the style, as it was with them all the while. Are you feeling me? They were forgetting to ask about the wealth, culture, innocence stolen and squandered, and our tradition that they sold, to the thieving one-door her. No, no such word was ever to be heard. But like, when they were to have wandered in and stolen, taking away precious things, good and golden. Even the food that they (the Lars) thought they would still have a lot of in the yards, and were emboldened. But in reality, they did not; that too was also stolen by the mad as f... The crooks would have taken away even that. Now that they have gotten all they would have gotten. Including the Bickle in the boiling pot of fat... um, food. After getting themselves really, really fat off the other guy's backside of the desert's hot... not good. It's now high time, it would seem, for them to be mean and to take and toss him in and away, hurt. To banish him to some other bay, in the dirt. Out there where he may stay and wither away in hurt and die.

"But, but, why?"

"How would I know? Go ask him, not I." One thing I do know, though. That was not to be the first time that he would have been doing him some time, you know. While rendering him blind, pretending to be kind, and acting kindly like that. It had gotten started way back then, way back in the days when he was young. His old man would have looked over the wind and would have heard of him. The Bungie one is who I'm talking about here, as in Stevens. Kingsley1 would have heard of Bungie Stevens and was glad. He sent for him, that said Steven, thing, because he wanted to have him come in unto them, to make leagues with them. "Mad." That right there, my friends, was the beginning of the pilfering. Good for them? Yes. But bad for him. Bad for them, and us too, bad for all of us in the end. Isn't that the awful truth?

"Yes."

Yet, what does that man do, the other one from the Larrie's crew? He waits for that special time of the year to go counting upon his counting pairs. He's always counting on him. Trying to justify the number of wonderful things that he and his Larrie kind companions are accomplishing, out of what they would have created and contributed to civilization, on the mountain. But not to his, just to the other folks' thriving society, and country over there on the grids (lie to me). The squares' civilization, in its bounty, was not his own. On and on we go a-counting, on the kids, not us. Huh-huh, look, he's still there, sitting upon his combo chair, and watching his bundle of nothingness grow and going nowhere.

"No, don't say that because it's not nice."

"Oh! Why not? What did you say? 'That's not nice,' was that what you'd said?"

"No, not really, but..."

"Oh, no, you're right, I'm sure." So, I offend you, right? How so? How is it then... how's it that it's the other men who tell you what to do, and where to go?' Gone out to sell you on what to go out and spend your money on, down the road. The same one who now gives you everything that you need, by truckloads. For a price multiplied by ice age degrees, no? Well, I suppose... For you to be able to give to the pickney dem, the wonders of the children's pen, so they may get a chance to go to school and learn how to write on other people's slate tools, just to be nice. Writing the right sin Ting, or the wrong ones. Yeah man, always writing some thin things, like the sum thing, yes. The words that they had never heard, and that was even while they were young and were our men's and women's beautiful children, and great with helping out our shepherds, no? When they were forced to go to steel tools instead of real schools. Even when they would much rather play with their friends in the streets and eat, then go off licking their fingers because the food was sweet. When my parents' rod was bent upon the backside of some of my best Larried friends' tents. On that very day, when we first were to have relented and gone out of the mercenaries' examination rooming tent without the proper spoon of consent to feed the rest of the argument, by noon. While on the journey into the future testament, in my room. My awe... soul would have felt it too.

"Suits you," he said and shot my boots instead. "Little brute you," he said, again. Cute, eh, cute. Amen. That right there, though, even though you and others like you may not be able to see or know. That was his key to dumping his strangeness on you and me. Go. Because our forefathers' eyes were not made too ready to see. Now, see? See what has come upon the Larrie family? You now do everything for everyone and their comfort, including them and him. Those who always come first, no sin. Look, my parents are now sparing the rod because of my acting mad and my bad mouth. Spewing a cup of tea all about, because he, yes, that other man, not Leigh, thinks that I'm not proper. So, he doesn't expect anything better from me (a disaster). But since I'm now his property working for share-cropper Leigh, he has surely got all the rights to come over and fix me up, tight, then go off to Ma's place to put the sugar in the cup of two teaspoons full of ice cream plight, please! What good is left of you and me? Can you even tell me? Turn your head around now and look at me, and be like, like, looking still. Come on, man, look, look at me, or be gone, out to sea. But what difference will it make anyway? Can you still see the day? Oh no, I know, it's not so. Forgive me, please, I'm in sorrow down on my knees. I'm sorry for speaking so, and for saying those very badly thought-out and half-full things, when everyone knows that it's not so, as all fools think. Who was it, though, who said that I'm a lying drying pool? I heard you, but please, allow me to "word you" with these. Things like this, and that. A word to the wise is a cool tool, well, so they say to a fool-fool, on the lot. But you can never talk sense to a four-legged stool, okay? They're chipping away at you even to this day. Digging away at your feet on the potter's clay, while you're out again, busy for the payday. "A man must get paid," you'd said, so you stay up late at night and work your faith and pray instead, by the bed of hay, where you oft lay your head. But as for them, and how they play? No, that's not their way. Other than for when they're going to sell it down the stairway, to folks such as me and you, okay?

"Okay."

Yeah. He isolates and takes out the best of you, then goes in and takes out your protesting friends, too. Just like they'd always done to folks like you back home. Yes, I know the gnome, that's his home, right over there. But that includes me too, the just comes. That's just his way, those things to do. That's how he plays, by his rules. Didn't he do it to the wild beast grazing out there on the plains of the grasslands feast? Yes, but that's nothing at all, I know, because they're just beasts. That's all, right? And you? Meanwhile, the rest of the pack looks on in shock, not having a clue as to what to do, or even to ask. Like, what do we make of that?

"What?"

"That, look!" What do we make of the whack attack? But look at this, and that. Look, nuh man, look at that. Popping your head up now, you stare out back and wonder, just like those out there on the wilder plains of the grasslands thunder used to do. You wonder why. "Why is this, and that?" You'd asked. Why the numbness in my spinal track? You would have reacted like that when you were forced to pack up and go back. Wow! Can you make the connection yet? Does it connect with you, my little pet? Have you seen yet on what to place a bet?

All the things that he made over and okay today, weren't good at all, just yesterday. Yet, in one lifetime, before overpopulation was a sign. They were filling your overtly uppity mind with their beautiful crime. But now, Four-letter words can freely be heard. To censor such is now deemed absurd. Freedom is a must, I know, now watch that freedom bus as it goes. Freedom of speech is the word to show, only don't ever tell someone what you think is right for their chow at the show. Nor talk about good gifts of sorts, such as a godly sieve, a spoon, or a fork. None such as these will ever work with the newly appointed smart. No, not for us, and you. Don't be nasty, sure, don't talk back, don't you ever put up a fight, or you'll be weed whacked. For sure, don't ever mention such freedom rights. Nonesuch as you might have once had and held tight. "It's bad and not to be allowed," so said the knights, and he's glad. But...

"Don't stop talking out of your freemen's mouths aloud," so said he, and rightly and fully so. Speak your truth in the streets, even out there in that timely crowd, go on out and do it and be proud. Such things are not censored anymore, not in this time of freedom of speech, adventures galore. Because freedom is a must, I know, it's for everyone and their pleasures to trust and show. Each of those who spoke these words, though, spoke only those things that are allowed to be spoken by him, and yes, you too, no?

"I don't know, I don't know."

Speak he them, though, even more so speak he about them, he said. He does them too, out there in the open view, in the public spheres. Even while his god is standing there, right by you, and he's fair. At the same time, the other man's rights are not as important a right as his rights are. Although those other rights are still there, dusting up the bills of wrongs... sorry, I meant to say, the bills of the right scars, of the day. But those are not his business, okay? No, they belong to the other man's kids. The Bungie one, for example, it was his fingers that were there upon the steel pulses of the pan... um air sample when those laws were being crafted over there, no? Yes, laws over which he often walked as dead, well, so I hear. Happened over there in the sphere of the squares, as said. Laws that were brought into being and came about by what he would have learned from the excursions in or out. By what was heard coming out of people's mouths, too, in his hearing, you know who. He'd learned these things when he went out there. Yes, he was made able to watch as people ran away from him, in fear. Or, when he'd sent those others out on the road route. He would have learned a lot from what they brought back home to him, in truth. Well, the rest of his men did, those who were in the group. Learned that people's mouths could be made to speak the code, yes, my youth. If they're nudged and prodded along the path toward such results. Even those codes that he would have written down in books, and placed in schools, and hence. Made him out to be another god, all about the town's end. He took note, then went out. But then, he came back in again and sat down and wrote. But how well did he live by those things? Take note; that's him — "That's the Bungie friend of theirs?"

"Yes."

"Well, just asking. But then again..."

As for them, those other modern men. Those freedom brigadiers and friends, look at them. They're doing it to us, too. No? Yes, they're doing those same kinds of things to you today, and on some of the other ones, too. Others, such as us and them, will be screwed right there and then. Even in the open view near the children's playpen. But as for the heathen, he then is the one who can't even have a chance to enjoy his right to live. But those who would have been the chief wrongdoers' friends last evening, while feeding his own needs to break the reed on which he was leaning, again. Even as it was done in the previous evening's prayer read while sitting with them, and breaking bread while eating. Before shooting his way out the doors, leaving many saints lying dead in the arms of the Lord on whom they were leaning for support. It is he, though, yes, he who polices the new legal biz and picks up the spent shells on the go. He's quick on the draw to let you know some things, like when he tells you such things as this: "You had better leave and go." That's what you're expected to do, no? Yeah, leave. Leave it up to him to teach you and the rest of them how to win. How to say, how to obey, and how to do. He will surely show you how to do what he wants you to do. He does the "say," and the show-and-tells, too. But it will be you who must do the "dos." But as for you? You may never do so, no. Not as you see him do. Unless it is to do...do, do those things that he tells and sells to you. Be sure to do those. Like, such new things. Never the old parts of those same legal arts and codes, though. Otherwise, the weight of the law will come down heavily on the backsides of your toes-oh. This is how we do things in this new age of freedom ring in which we now live, and are quick to forgive, quietly forgiving everyone but that one over there where you live. He who'd dared to do me wrong by going about refusing me my rights. Because he seems to think that what I have fought for and have gained the right to do is not righteous enough or true. He now seems to think it's okay for him to deny me my pay, but by going about it in the "right" way. He'll soon see what shall become of him tonight, or even right away. I'm going to make him pay with all of his might, and with all that I can take away from him, even his sight. Then, when I'm done, I'll throw him into the dustbin, dunk him under the lid, and cover him in. Got to teach him a thing or two, so that he will learn and get to know a new truth. Don't go messing around with the law, which is the law. Although it may be new, and cannot be changed at all. Nah. These great things were to come popping up against my eye-skins, would have happened and come to pass only after "we," (meaning them, they) would have had to fight hard to change that old and outdated card. Had to exchange the strange and would have re-arranged it to suit "us," and to fit it into the names of the lords, and our priest and profits, to collect and send over to our prophets. After we had gone in and had them do the amendment bits. Fixing whatever part of it was recommended by me to be amended. For the sake of my outfit, too, the courtesy was extended. So that they can't do that sort of thing to us ever again, as men did. Now they want to come and dictate those old-fashioned mistakes and blabber-mouthed debates on me, and at my front door gate too, turning the key. They will soon see what we shall do to them to make them understand that they cannot go around do-ing things like that to people. Not people like us. Not in this free man's freedom vehicle.

"Not on this blinking bus."

"No, don't do that, don't even go near to cuss. We've got to maintain calm and give them no cause for alarm, for us to keep the bus moving along, onward, forward to the final freedom chant."

Meanwhile, "That's impossible," said the young security supply guy in a style. "Huh, yeah! I hear what you say, but. What's impossible about it, hey?" He hissed back at the prophet. "I just said it, shush, didn't I? So, if I did speak those very words, and I can see that you've heard me, clearly. What then is the 'impossible' part of the whole thing?" Or were you trying to make a liar out of him? Meaning, was he trying to say that nobody said anything big or small? Nothing like that, to him at all? What do you say, Paul?

...

The bicycle debacle. "Watch the ride," he said. Can't lie to you, Clyde, mi bred. It did hurt me deep within my side, shed. Yeah, that ride was what caused it, as said. It's like, like, that thing that he took and hid from me when he did the thing that he did. I was careful about it when I did it, you know. But I had to go. I'd forgotten what was about to happen. I forgot to lock it up properly when I parked it. It would have been to my sorrow that I did it, to my grandma's kid. I only intended to borrow and hide it, you know, like the little boy's bicycle, and ride it, just for spite, until tomorrow, and I did. Like, maybe until tomorrow night when I could return it on a barrow. But it was like, like, it's a dope bike, alright? So, I didn't bother to take it back at all last night. After all, the kid was small, and his parents were really rich, Paul. Richer than Richler Hall, I'm telling you, man. That bicycle was really cool, too. But then came those fools; the two crooked, thieving, no-good deadheads from quitting school. That is their favorite tool, it would seem to me. To go around and take other people's carefully crafted barstools that weren't given to me, and any other thing that might be cruel, you see. They took my bike the other night, and that could never be right, no matter how one chooses to look at it. It was a nasty, dirty act from a bunch of doggish crooks, that's it. Man, I feel so violated. Crooks are underrated; they don't seem to know and understand the pain and anguish that they tend to place on someone's handgrip. Which was, in fact, just that. It was there among the things that they'd grabbed and run off with, took it off the handle of the bike where it was fastened to firm up one's grip. Oh, sheet! man! What pain the rightful owner of the thing was to have felt, when they handled it and ran away with stealth, like that bicycle bike thing in proper, that's what he had felt, I mean, me. That was what I would have felt, too, my papa. Just, just for example, I'm using this sample. But the bicycle, though. That bicycle that they hitched on a ride, and then came back inside and took that same night to leave and go, like, really? They just take it away as if it belonged to them; they, and not me. Hey! It isn't fear, man, it wasn't their belongings. But there's surely coming a day when people like them are going to be caught plumb in on the runnings and are going to be made to pay. But until that day comes. I'm left here to just walk away, or run, since my bike is now in their hold to stay. Ah, um! I'm left here to foot it along, all the way. Man, that is so, so very wrong.

Today, in an environment of overpopulation, as it is. They're manipulating us (people like you and me) down a hazardous, slanted vent, through the sieve. Designed, it would seem, to multiply the number of escape routes to get you out of here clean, like in dreams, but to their suit. "While I'm generally biased towards agreeing with the view that the earth is finite, and maybe, staring at its limits, plight." Well, so said the old man, yes, said that same old man to the one on his right. "I don't think there is any equity in them deciding on which one, and targeting who they think it is that should stay versus who the dogs should bite on the booted bottom, or who should go hopping along tonight. Not that it ought to be so, no. It's not about one or the other, it's about each man as my brother," he said. "However, if you're there with your head in the sand, and will not take a stand in working out a plan to pave the way for moving on, to your benefit? Then, you're probably the right one to get out of it. From here, to go up and over, like, over there, at the very least of bones."

They're messing with our children's lifeline. But some of us cannot seem to see the signs because it's happening in the side view of our messed-up blinds, you know? Like, the blind spot kind of mind. But mind you, Will. You've got those two eyes still. Be sure to start blinking them in line with the times, and that is going to be best if done before you can even think about a reproduction thought line. Because they're building a new ark design, to set out sailing down the timeline. It's called sperm banking, Steine. This was designed, it would seem, to ensure that something is left behind, just in case you know. If after he's done with destroying the thyme, and the better traces of the Hughman's races, to go, such as thine. If he then noticed that he'd missed a sign, as in this case. So it is about to be, no denying it. He thinks that he will still have something else to fall back on and be able to try backing up and in again, Aunt Sue. To retrace his steps and remake anything that he might have wasted in haste. Anything that he may then find out that he could do well with, in his behind-the-scenes kind of space. To go mixing in with the mistake, just to get things back a little, or even a lot, like they were before. Better that one, and more, than... Or as close to it as he may be able to drag back in, through the door, jam...

Meanwhile, while the Lars were there doing more of their nothing, my star. Nothing other than plotting sand and stoning the wind with "har", I mean, her. Squares were working, not just sitting up there upon his hind sin Ting, and jerking, half a pound of pork and chickens. He was and still is busy, very busy indeed. Busying himself with plotting and planning his ways to protect his place in the continuum, dizzy, Ingrid. Lars said that they will go far, because they are from ancient times and the first bar, yeah! Of course, they are. On a musical scale, perhaps. "Strong from birth too," back a rock where he was when he said this, "and will live out the curse of the bat brutes."

"Or was it Al Davies' fault?"

"Mi nuh knuoh at all, my youth, I don't know man."

Squares, though, do know a thing or two. Like, what they ought to do to cull and control me and you, so as not to saturate the growing waste nor allow the nuisance to overrun the space. He, too, had fallen asleep once upon a long time. But then, upon one of his waking-up-again signs, he'd turned his eyes to look around and found that he was outnumbered in kind and lagging way behind.

"No problem, friend of mine, I've still got the time." So said that squared Kingsley, king divine.

"Summon up the general," he instructed the corporal. We've got lots of work to do here. Can't allow Larrie's feet to overrun our shoe on the square. Blow the bugle, strike up the bands. Come, let's go wipe out the bunch of them off the face of the KD's Kingsland. And it came to pass. Yes, Larry was taken to task. Look, as it is this day, they're still nursing the loss and running away, fast. But lo and behold, the story was told, and the outcry from the fields was fast and cold. The job is done, go and spread the word, Squares can and have already put away the sword. But not too far and perhaps, not for long. It's lying dormant somewhere close at hand. Squares will not be done until all and everything is in his hands. As everyone already knows, those squares never go anywhere. You're reading this now; he's reading it too, so tell me, what do you think he's going to do? Isn't it in his ways, the tried, tested, and true, to go out and do things for others before they do you? Or was it: do unto others before they do the screw unto you? Or some other thing like that. One can't always remember a lot. Yet you say it isn't true, so you sit there just like you have always been known to do; leave your gate swinging and keep it wide open. Let him walk right on in because you're hoping. You believe in things as you have long been known to do, Hingh. You believe that it's some more goodies that Santa is bringing. So, you opened the door and let him walk right in last evening. When he leaves this time, there will be no further sign of anyone closing the door behind... Like, closing the gate behind him. For goodness' sake, remind them, don't make that same mistake. Oh no, wait. Is it already too late?

This is going to hurt a little, I know, or a lot, maybe so. But I've got to say it anyway, and send it along and over to Joe. Just because, and just this once. Never repeat it ever, never again, or else... Here goes. "Money to work." That's it. Now say it quickly and quit. Say it like this: don't get money to work for you. Ever. It's a bad, bad thing to do, brother. I'm a-pointy-fingering as I'm warning you, don't do it, or else. That's it. Now, quit. From my "love letters to my Black brothers" collection.

Since we're already there, here are some more wet paint psyches for your listening ear. Don't ever correct those children; let the correctors correct you and tell you how to let them loose, so that he may overkill them, and crush them with his boots, to his suits.

What else did you expect? It's me again, wagging my finger at you, my friend, pointing the blame just the same. Don't ever do it, that stinking thinking thing. Let me walk you through it, like, such things as the thinking sin. It's like. It's bad, bad, slapping the wrist like Dad.

Squares, scared and cruel as he is, he will not duel unless, and until... Well, not until the back of the vest that is wearing his guests is the openest of spaces, and open to more of his best, as in his best interest, such a thing may come to be, as this case is. But with that said, don't just go to bed and lie down in restful sleep. As for him, he never sleeps, remember?

He's still there, plotting whips and planning what's coming next. Like, coming down the pipe to bite you on the neck tonight, so again I say to you. Don't sleep tight, ever.

Remember what happened to them back then? He came in when he first came in, took the trees to make them paper-thin. Then made it some more, added vapor phlegm, and varnished it up with vanishing cream. See what I mean? Yeah! Soon, payment on parchment will mean pay un-parr, like cement. Then, your payment will be gone, and so too will the family farm. Just like the lands of your forefathers are all gone, shipped off to the production line of the other man, as the first step of his plans. Now, though, we've got paper money won, Vin, all packed in and done. Yes, man, me, you, they, and them. All of us, again, among other such glistening things. But then again. We're about to see those signs of the same old timely outcome crimes, signing in. Look, now it's all gone to squares from him, yeah! From them. Like, Lars obeys on the ends. In return, they're craving spare change with the same old pay on par, as in a paper money jar. As if that's the most valuable thing on earth, there are or ever will be. But as for me? Look...

The man of old was to dust off his soul and pick up again the scroll. As he was about to push back at the bulge in his eyes, he watched his jawbone take a tumble and roll. All because of what he was told when they had to tell him some things, such as these…

16

Jamming in the Jan Can

Now we're jamming, jamming. Jamming in the jam can and fanning. "Boy! Is it hot in here or what? What have we got here?" He queried the ask over his beer, slurring the words off the place where his tongue used to be heard, yes, there. But now, he just needs to do a little peek, like, to go take a sneak peek at pee-peeping in the lavatory. "Here," he was heard to swear, "hold this for me," he said, it's his can of beer. "I'll be right back," said the man, and then, he was a lot gone, just like that.

"What's taking him so long, though?" Asked the boy, now still holding on to the can, "No!" Yes, he can no longer hang on to this beer-can-watching plan, so he had to hop along to go knock upon the Jan, or more like, upon the door of the pan, and much, much more than... No score, man, no response came back to dance at the banging dooring circumstance. So, he pushed, was pushing hard up against the bush, sorry Flore, I meant to say, upon the door. As you already know the score, people don't bother to push the bulls-hit anymore, therefore. He would have pushed the door open and stepped right in. Into what he thought was a forgotten sin ting, or something. The dude had forgotten to hit the light by switching it on before he went off to do the pissing rite, he thought. "Right?"

"Well, I suppose so."

"No, he was wrong." He was falling through the darkness, headlong. Down, down, down look, he's going down. But then came the sound of the sudden stop. Luckily for him, it was to hit upon a splash, and the breathing was to hit him once again, softer than the goner that he thought had come upon him, at the end. Now, look, he's in the swim; lots of others are there with him. Yelling, shouting, and clawing away at getting to them, yeah, up there where they stay, seated. In the exalted place above where we did...

"You're kidding, kid, right?"

"No. I'm not; this right here was the actual act." We were there, way down below; they were up there on top of the bough, you know? Upon the rain-bowed-circled seating area above the fighting flow. Those in the water below didn't know, though, that there were yet other eyes looking on. Looking at them and us, and watching all that was going on on the tarmac, and all the happenings in the pond.

"Whose eyes were those?"

"Questions to find answers for, I'd supposed, and went off obeying the codes, but that's what the rest of us were doing there that day; fighting." We were fighting our way to getting it to those men on the high end. To go give to them what was coming, and still is, it's coming to them, even now. Speaking of coming, another person just came dropping in like a cow. Did you not hear that, the mowing and screaming? He came dropping in through the same crack I'm in, I mean, through the very same dark hole that catapulted me in. I'm now getting the feeling as if that's how we all got here, leaving behind us a whole fountain of beer. Now, here we are again, in the den. All men, yes, none of those others with them, you know them, those woe — "Whoa, wait a minute. Those who?"

"The woe men, you know them, no?"

"No, don't do that to them, or else that thing will surely come upon you again. Like, like the 'woe' one that you were just about to spew in on them." But no, we're talking about some rather beautiful women here, go. Take a look and see if you don't believe me, and stare. Meanwhile, look up there on the ballroom floor with those beautiful tiles covering the nook. The party is as haughty as before. Wearing away at those shoes in styles, I'm sure, even as a book. But every now and then, there goes another one of the men. You know them, they've got to go do their thing when they're out doing other things, such as the drinking, sin Ting, things, for example, just for example.

The restroom door says "Gentlemen," so. That was where they usually went to do the go thing, you know? When a man has got to go, he's got to go. So, one by one, they would have gone, and went... Not to be returning ever again. Well, at least not yet, and not in the same way they went in, whereby they would have gotten wet. Something was cooking down there in the kitchen. That would have been near and dear to the place where each man would have fallen. Or more like, somewhere there in the peripheries of those drop-in centers, was the kitchen's door to enter. An answer to the call, yes, that's what it was, from the higher-up callers, with love, to the gentler... Those who were down there, somewhere a little lower than the ballroom shoulder. Getting cold and yet much colder. Well, they were cold altogether, not just those at the bottom and in the water, but those at the header also. They were surely colder, yes, mi bredda, well, so said my beloved brother. They were colder, somewhere between each one's shoulders.

"How cold were they anyway?"

"How cold," you'd asked my soul mate. Grab hold of your soul tighter than the platter there in your hand on the plate. Do this as the new task, eh, because. You're about to growl at what is about to unfold on your ah..." Never mind. Dinner time is almost here, but before we get to the Tupperware, some more dropping in are about to be happening down there in the darkroom — Boom! Boom.

"What's that sound? Does this spell doom, for some?"

"No, not yet, but... um" When the smoke was cleared, and they could look upward... Well, not really, they could have always looked wherever they wanted to, including up in that little nook with you. But that didn't mean that they were going to be able to see what they were looking up there to see. Because the smoke from the boom blast had darkened the entire room very quickly, meaning fast. Well, it wasn't even a room to speak of. Just an oval-shaped dome looking somewhat like that. Yes, like the belly of a thermos home, but cold alone, not hot. One that (mercifully) had a deep pool of water inside, at the time. Which was there to serve as a breaker line to break up the full fall of all those who took the tumble in and after, and wide. Unaware though they might have been when going in, they were in and could not seem to be able to find a way out again. Other than the way that their "host," those who were sitting there on a platform several arm's span above the water spouts, were. As for them, they were made very aware, I'm sure. Up there, where they were and looking on, the floor.

They were sitting up there and looking over the goings-on downstairs in the pond. But as for us, we were down there on the narrow ledge on which we were all evening, standing and begging, as if for bread and leggings. Now, though, we're soaked, cold, and scared stiff out of our bandwidths. Hostages were we, like this, standing there and nursing our shaking knees, and begging for our lives properly. With please, please, and yet more, please. But as for those knives? Look, the knives are sharp and short, as I'm able to tell by that person's reaction after thumb-testing the edge of the blade in his claw... But the night is long and is about to get longer. At last, there seemed to be a cut-off point in the age ranges of those men in the can, there. In the minds of those deranged, yes, beware, of the selective selecting clan; the weak-spined... Better that, though, than the man. "You know what I am... right? Like, like, what I'm talking about, right?"

Yes, as it pertains to the cutting plan, I think, but still "Yes?" Yes, that's how it was to go. Although they (same as you) didn't know, let's do you a bit of tell-and-show. Ahead of them was the cut-off point at which a different fate was to befall them. Those young, well, let's just say younger, as we'd like to call them, gentlemen. The younger men, those who would have been about twenty-five years old and under, below them, were sent to one side of the room, all the rest to another. Then, those young men on this side over here would have ended up serving tables as waiters on the ballroom floor for the night. Starting mere moments after they were initiated in the workings of such things and given their queues, to fright-night. As for the others, the older men and fathers, they were to serve too, and be served, yes. As well as being served up.

"Oh! Shuts!" Well, not all of them, or more like, not all parts of them, just that part. They were all given a choice, you know. "The jewels," they say, "or your lives," like, I mean, the real jewels, like, the real kinds of family jewels. Yeah! That kind of jewel. You do know where that was going to lead, don't you? Yes, they would have to duel. Because no man was going to be that quick on the gift when it comes to that kind of giving. The gift-giving on the shilling? No, not that willing, Mister Gilling, so they were going to have to fight it out. But that battle would have been won by... not the other side, but the one. You know him, the one who's with the upper hand. As always, he's the one who always wins, as for him? He would have been sitting up there on the stand all along. Very well-rested by now and in command, still holding on to the strength of his brand. Each of the others, though, was wasted after the waterfall that he would have tasted down below, and the time being so long on which he had to bear with it. Standing there upon the plank, and the promises. Just hanging on to it, sometimes. Or tumbling around and rolling on and off the ledge, at other times, with a mouthful of begging and a pledge to do as the man had said. "Just get me through and out of this strange twist of fate," he said. She who would have been mere moments before, lying with you, him, or someone else there, in bed, I'm sure. Yeah, that would be Fate, as said. But their hosts were twisted men of wit, so as the negotiations were to go on, the gift? They agreed to give up the garden seeds. But only in return for the man in need, and then, into the kitchen, they were to proceed... like, they proceeded to go. Then came the other men, the younger ones under them. It's now time to go and take commands from the real men in command and go wait on those tables all night long. Now! What such delicate and exotic treats, the women are so delighted to eat! Look at this! Served up on a blazing platter with bitter herbs was the meat. In the presence of a hundred and seventy of each man's chosen women folks, like nerds, to take and eat, to begin with. They were sitting there with them, yes. The spouses of those mutilated dimwits, those distinguished gentlemen that I'm with, were there. At the end of the evening, though, half of those women remained. Because every time one of those women was to have winced, grimaced, or gasped at the reveal of what the contents of the meal she would have managed to taste were. She was eliminated by the method of choice, as seen through those dimwits' eyes. Leaving for them there, several pots full of rice, without them tasting even so much as a single bite of it. Therefore, only the bravest, coldest, or most talented actors amongst the women there in party dress were to remain atop the stained-up fortress, at the end of the day, I swear. Not just that night but the day, as things were to be from that day on. What do we do now, with them, with what remained of those women?

Note: Take your emotions out of the mix and just read the writing scripts. That's it. Now sit, as we go right back into doing it, to them. But how was it going as it applies to those serving servers, since they would have been privy to some knowledge greater and further? This one over here might know a thing or two about that, because... He was there walking the ballroom floor and passing again by the restroom door. The same one through which he had tumbled and fallen before. Now, though, lucky for him, he's not down there anymore; he's back there walking on the better floor, doing the rounds, and serving. Somewhere nearer to the kitchen than the dive-in. One hand now bearing the silver platter. His other hand is pretending as if it wasn't proper... like as if it wasn't properly guarding the family jewelry for him and his papa. At the same time, the knees wobbled below the pea... soup. As they approached each table where the high and mighty men, not to be so mighty ever again, were. "Yeah, ease it in, with the scoop, look." They were to be sitting there on each man's chair above their knees. Or more like trying. Trying hard to sit atop the scarred parts, near the peas. But they were men who also happened to be the fathers of several of those shaky-kneed waiter friends of ours. Yes, those over there, and these. They were sitting there, very uncomfortable in the chair. Waiting to try and devour each man's most reluctant meals ever, since they must; it was a part of the timely trust that they were made to sign as surety to find another time walking atop their every man's grave line, like, atop the dust. Hence, they took hold of a fat chance at preserving what was left of their tentative lives. But how about husbanding the bandings with their wives? Is this going to be the end of that Thrive? Go ask Clive, he might know. But seriously, though, things are about to go down another sieve. They, yes, them; those same twisted wits of men. They are the very ones who are left up there to do the shake-up and the shares and to give. They're there, even now, thinking up another place in which we're to live. For all the natives of this Kingsland world, all-inclusive.

At the end of the planning, here comes the end of their problem; a new way of doing things was being attempted, where one would see things, like me, the norms and customs of the distant to the immediate past, changed and done away with at last. Because they're being turned on their heads, and fast. A new world is being born even now at their cost. Not some other world from somewhere else, not as an as...!

But this present Kingsland world", they'd said. As done over and a lot better for everyone. A place where, when negotiating, we negotiate with the idea that: He who takes the knife to the apple, it is he who gets to pick his cut last. Like, at the bottom of the bottle, like, the dregs in the glass. So, if you are that person, and let's say. You're sitting there on yourrrrass-tafar-I, and it is you who is sitting at the table and making the rules, like, the one who is to decide each man's portion, even in the pools. You will then get your chance to pick your piece of the apple pie, but after everybody else. Even he, yes, him and I, yes, mi cous. In so doing, they say, you're more than likely to be fair in apportioning the shares in the sharing, that way. This is to take effect after the jubilee that will follow each night of the family jewelry, to be the chance that we've long waited for, where everyone gets to start afresh and with no debt load to carry over the bar when we jump on the lorry on the way there, to go and see her. Imagine a new reality. Imagine a Kingsland world where men truly live in peace and equity. A place where this man helps and encourages the other one to become his best self, where what this one does well will complement what the other one does well, for the ultimate good of all. A place where, if this person hurts, that one feels the pain. Just like a line from a well-known song said it very eloquently once again: How high will the sycamore grow? If you cut it down, you will never know... Adopted, not mine. But this is to become the new mantra in this new place, phase, and cultural pastime. Let's see the other extremes of the possibilities upon your face and much more if you task me with doing mine. Such as afore-times, we've never seen, let alone tasted. Let those Sycamores grow, see what I mean? Instead of this man grabbing the spoil from that one, after he was done with killing him, and all the possibilities that might have been lying dormant within him. Or even those that he was in the process of working on, last evening, or at the time when that other man fell on him and killed him. Because he thought that, "There's no good in him. He's better off dead," so he said, and so too is the world's equilibrium. It too will be better off without him, sleeping there in peace in his permanent bed, in the Loom. Not to mention the resources that he was sitting on over there, in my room, and doing nothing with. It is surely going to be more valuable to us, in this thieving man's possession, to sit than it was in his hands. Yet, the beat goes on. But does it? Does it have to be that way, or is there another? Like, is there another, like, better way, my brother? Just asking for a friend who needs to hear...

The Conclusion

As the sun began to set on the battlefield, the sound of clashing swords and battle cries slowly faded away. The two warring factions had been locked in a deadly conflict for years, decades, even. With neither side willing to back down. But now, after countless battles and the loss of lives, the end was finally in sight. Both sides were exhausted and depleted by this; their armies were decimated, and their resources stretched to the limit. In a last-ditch effort to end the conflict, the leaders of the two factions met on the battlefield, in the middle of it. They stood facing each other, their eyes locked in a tense stare-down. For a moment, it seemed as though the tension between them would never break, in a slow dance. But then, slowly but surely, the two leaders began to lower their weapons (toward me lying on the ground). At first, the soldiers on both sides were hesitant to follow suit. "Oh, Shoo! I almost crap my... oops." But as they saw their leaders sheathe their swords like this, Shreesh, and extend their hands in peace, over my boots. They, too, began to lay down their arms, and after years of bitter conflict, the war was finally over, in truth. The two factions had agreed that they would work together towards a brighter future for all, as free men. As the soldiers on both sides began to embrace and exchange heartfelt apologies, it was clear that a new era had dawned, towards this: a time of peace and cooperation, where the wounds of the past could finally begin to heal. As the sun dipped below the horizon, the leaders of the two factions shook hands, each promising to do their part in building a better tomorrow for all. The war may have been long and brutal, but now, it was time for a new beginning for the two pals. As the dust settled on the battlefield, the two warring factions faced each other one last time, but this time, they shook hands again.

It had been a long and bitter war, with both sides suffering heavy losses and enduring unimaginable hardships. But now, it was finally over. So, the two sides came together in a tentative truce. There were still wounds to heal and scars to bear, but for the first time in years, there was hope for a better future. Over the following weeks and months, the two factions worked together to rebuild their shattered world. They set aside their differences and learned to cooperate and collaborate in ways they never thought possible. As the years passed, the old grudges and grievances began to fade away. The once-bitter enemies who became friends, then allies, began working together to create a better world for their children and grandchildren. The war that had once threatened to tear their world apart was finally over. It had been a long and difficult journey, but in the end, it was worth it all. Because, out of the ashes of the old conflict, a new and better world had been born, which leads us towards this.

The end of a trilogy.

Here for you is an excerpt from our next-in-line project; a book called "Collect Calls." A collection of short stories and poems from this pen of mine. Don't miss it at all.

Lead sheet into tug life.

They were friends and playmates, less than a day separating them from being the same age. One could scarcely separate them in the early days. Sigismund and Welton grew up together there on the island. Welton migrated to North America with the wild one, the other half of the timely twins, known to us as Welton and him, remained on the square, changed his name somewhat there, and ended up in a gang. Leading it along. Sporting guns and cars, and girls as you are, and flashing cash. Tainted cash for sure, and lots of it to help him score. Then came that fateful day when Welton, the expatriate friend from a long time gone, returned home to spend time burying a close family member and a friend of mine, guess who showed up again, asking for financial favors from him, like handouts and such other things? Yes, Big Sig it was, Sigismund the tug. Siggy wasn't asking for handouts because he was cash-strapped and in doubt, like, needing a helping hand up and getting out, no, it was just the way things were done. Big Sig runs things around this neck of the hooded town now, and if you're to be even so much as passing through town on the way to Sunday school, as it was known. Chip the switch and enforces his rules in his town, and is careless enough to pass under Siggy's radar up the slide rule bar. Don't be found skidding back down the hot tar. You had better be sure to have enough dough in your pocket row to pay the toll, at the get-go. Otherwise, be prepared to pass up on this week's quota of blessings from the hand of the Lord. Because she most definitely won't be receiving this week's incremental installments to pay the rent on such. Nor for the daily feeding, not at your handling arms' length. It will be gone over to care for the needs of Brother Sigismund's car and spent, and that's all. As is now the case with Welton. She most definitely won't be receiving that one, from them, or whatever else the pay-up name would have meant. It's not going to be forthcoming this time, no, not at your hands, Welton. So Welton was in for a rude awakening from his slumbering journey. What transpired from there is the stuff that makes for a thrilling story, such as is just about to be seen happening over there near Ghearny, where he used to live.

Welton handed off a handful of bills, trying to buy his way out of the sure bloody spills. The spilling of his migratory blood, if you will. Good enough to buy himself a free pass, this time. But he'd better be gone quick before Big Sig gets to find out that those bills weren't the real free-flowing kind. They were specific to a particular shopping store line. Some sort of reward to get one coming back the next time, but. Welton was long gone when Siggy found out what his friend had paid him to spend. Look at his reaction when he got home into the light and started counting it out that night, again. He was as mad as hell and swore that Welton had better not come back, or else. But he did, and that was when these things began to happen, on the skid.

It started much earlier on. Welton was privy to witnessing a dusting in the early days, like, in front of our very eyes, yes, before he'd gazed on him, and me. Was to have happened when Siggy shook the lunch money out of Sean's stonewashed jeans and walked away with the entire sunny means. Sean had to then lie his way out of another bout of beating and dusting of sorts. All at the hands of his own sweet and dear loving father's lusting parts. "For what?" you'd asked. For losing his lunch money to a group of boys, or another such disgusting ploy. Surely not to just one very well-known kid named Big Sig.

Welton was in for another rude awakening on his next return trip home from foreign. What happened there is the stuff that makes up for this thrilling story here, and to go and share the comments when he gets back down off the air. Well, if. But he didn't know squat about that and this, as it was to have turned out.

Three degrees higher than yesterday, the heat has gotten up on the wrong side of the bed again today. Even in the shadow of the Poinciana tree, she felt as if she was bread in the oven baking patties for tea. Shannon could see the motorcycle approaching from half a mile down the road, peddling his wares and trading, coming now towards them. Of course, it was him. Fudgy was riding his motorbike towards them, seated there in front of the luscious load, as usual. She was quick to see him because she was standing at the half-open gate since, since... Just a little school gal, you know. The reluctant gate itself was resting on her backside all the while, while she was waiting, and looking out for him. As coming things were prone to be done, and as shown on this very evening. She had been looking all morning long, and into the afternoon song too. Readying herself to go about singing a sweet, showering refrain on you. Trying to see a sign of the ice cream man walking the line and coming on through. Or more like, riding. Riding his bike into view, just to get things she likes a lot, all settled in rightly, and not running headlong into you. At the same time. She was in the middle of praying. Yes, praying that today is going to be a good day's win, for her, of course, not him. She was praying that her mother was going to be a bit richer today than she was yesterday. Most importantly, richer than she was the last time, when the ice cream vendor of class and flying high, had happened to walk the lined path in and to pass by this way. That would have been last week at this same time of day. She was hoping then, too, with the same outcome on which to chew; nothing. However, she's super optimistic still. Hoping that her mama will be able to get her something soft and sweet, out of that fudgy miracle box of his. "Cool nuh man, just chill." The one that he carries behind his back on the motorbike, and which usually contains the creamy, delightful goodness that she likes and craves all the time. But can only hope to get a sign of some of the time. Like, more or less like when Santa pops into town at Christmas time. Yeah, man, you know what! That Santa friend of mine tends to be kind and caring like that. As for Fudgy and Mama's lucky charmer, though? Not so much so. Quite unlike how things are with some other superstar, as may be seen happening now with that Savia friend of hers, and me. Savia, Shannon's best friend to her, from the savior. Look, look at her and her misbehavior there again. She's dancing and skipping away gleefully at the hind side of her mother's lovely backside and hugging her waist above the bow-legged knee pulley now. Oh boy, wow! That woman is blessed, yes. Was born with a golden spoon wedged up somewhere between her jaw, they say, and so far, all the evidence is bending towards supporting those claimed bear paws, okay? But now, look at her; she's standing up for the right of the good name there again, you know. Center-staged between the ice cream vendor and Skipadidoo dancing, Savia. She whose fingers and thumb were just a moment ago merrily and brightly rampaging through that purse of her mother's and hers. Searching for the exact change I'd supposed, to pay the ice cream salesman or fudgey the fee, for the tax man and me. Whichever one of those names one may choose to call him, half-heartedly. The choice of name is probably going to be dependent on which treat from the box excites you more, in fact. That will probably be the deciding factor in which of those names one may choose to place on his door frame from the box, no? No, not on the door frame but, but on the head of the ice cream vendor and village clown. The man who's riding the cycle with the motor and coming on down is the same cycling salesman. Look, it's coming up behind her; that's for sure the proper way to score. On any given day on Caymanas' shore, he could be more. On one day, he may be fudgy, but on the next, he could just as easily be creamy. That's what Shannon is going to call him today after feeling me. That's it for this excerpt. Coming soon: COLLECT CALL.

"Note from the author"

Just a note of thanks for choosing to read my book and for sticking with the story. You must have liked it a lot. At this point, I want to ask you, my reader, to take a minute or two to post a review of the book on the Sales pages at Amazon and/or any other such sales pages. This small gesture is so very much appreciated. So, go ahead, slap a hit on the subscribe butt below, and show the vine some love. And don't keep it to yourself; be sure to share this. I thank you.

More notes: some lines and quotes in this book may be recognized as familiar lines from some well-known (or not-too-well-known) songs. We lay no claim to the ownership of these materials and only use them out of pure love and admiration for the pieces and, in some cases, the authors. Should the rights owners have issues with our usage of any of these pieces, just let us know, and we will make the necessary efforts to rectify the situation and/or remove the offending pieces, after verifying the authenticity of the claim, as is very possible nowadays. Thank you very much.

Special thanks to these people who have helped in various ways in bringing about this book. Thanks to my immediate as well as extended family: To Leonie and Charles, who had to put up with me not being quite there at times, even when I might have been there in body. In the end, your support was unwavering and unmistakable. Thank you. To my extended family who supported me by allowing me time, space, and also physical support, by spending your hard-earned cash to purchase the books, or by telling others about them. To Giulia and Paul, especially. I thank you ever so much.

So why do I write, did you ask?

The answer is this: I'm a guy of many words, but my tongue is slow and heavy, and my words tend to come out awkward and clumsy, so I write because I always have something to say. Which always tends to get me into trouble anyway. The extra bonus in writing is that a pencil usually comes with an eraser.

About Us

E Lloyd Kelly is an Author, poet, and songwriter. Born in Jamaica, West Indies, to Raglan and Alma Kelly. Now resides in Montreal, Quebec, where (when not writing,) he drives a shuttle bus between campuses at McGill University.

If you haven't yet done so. Be sure to read book 1. A story called "New Hiking Trail, Cast Shadow on the Tattooed." And:

Book 2, "Twisted Tales from the Big Fail." Available wherever books are sold. If you can't find it, ask them to get it for you.

Coming soon: Collect Calls. Be on the lookout.